Portal to E'ewere

BOOKS BY IRMA WALKER

Inherit the Earth
Portal to E'ewere

Portal
to E'ewere

by

Irma Walker

An ARGO Book

ATHENEUM *New York*

1983

My thanks to Elnora C. King
for the words for Aur'ri Song

LIBRARY OF CONGRESS CATALOGING IN PUBLICATION DATA

Walker, Irma   Portal to e'ewere.

"An Argo Book"
SUMMARY: *In a crowded uncompromising future world,*
a girl seeks a visionary place of space and beauty,
and just when she seems to succeed,
she is confronted with a terrible choice.
[1. Science Fiction]   I. Title.
PZ7.W1529Po   1983   [Fic]   83-2634
ISBN 0-689-30998-8

Copyright © 1983 by Irma Walker
All rights reserved
Published simultaneously in Canada by
McClelland & Stewart, Ltd.
Composition by
American Book-Stratford Graphics, Brattleboro, Vermont
Printed and bound by
Fairfield Graphics, Fairfield, Pennsylvania
Designed by Mary Ahern
First Edition

To EMILIE JACOBSON: *with deep gratitude*

FOREWORD

(Excerpt from *Middle Years: A Look at World/ Earth Between the Age of Chaos and New Birth;* Jeremiah T. Bishop, Director of World/ Earth History Studies, Five Worlds University, New America City, World/ New Birth; published by Five Worlds University Press, Year 408 After Chaos.)

"... and so World/ Earth in the middle of the Twenty-First Century, Anno Domini, was in a state of near anarchy. Many factors contributed to the over-crowding, the hedonism, the rampant crime and racial violence, the breakdown in religious mores and familial ties, but the end result was the disintegration of society as a whole.

As a result of a rash of civil and so-called "brush fire" wars (see *brush fire wars:* Glossary of Terms) hordes of refugees from the Third World nations (see *Third World nations:* Index) poured into the affluent, industrialized countries of World/ Earth. When ordinary policing methods were ineffectual against the onslaught of refugees, those nations sealed their borders and retreated into isolation, a process that still continued two centuries later at the time of New Birth.

Because of its location and its thousands of miles of border, the United States of America, North America's dominant and most powerful nation, was particularly vulnerable to the waves of refugees from the South American and Caribbean civil wars. When the country became ungovernable from its single control center on the Eastern Coast (see *Washington, D.C.;* Glossary of Geographic Names), a series of smaller nations evolved, each autonomous, each pursuing its own methods of survival.

In the strongest of the new nations, the N'Eastern States of America, a council of nine men, drawn from government, the military, science, industry and the clergy, met to formulate a new order, a behavior code flexible enough to be accepted readily by its citizens, yet strong enough to withstand the tides of anarchy.

Borrowing from philosophy, from human psychology studies and various religious disciplines, from military intelligence mind-control techniques (see *brain washing practices;* Glossary of Terms), the Council of Nine devised a system of behavior mores they called the Courtesy Code.

Originally the Code was intended as a temporary stopgap measure until such time as technology could solve the problems of over-population.

But the Council of Nine had done its job too well.

By Year 191 After Chaos, the new order was so well-entrenched that any speculation about change, even in scholarly terms, was considered a crime against the State. In a society so overcrowded that even the word *privacy* had come to mean the right to protect one's self against the stare of another citizen, the technology that was to find solutions to overpopulation was now totally committed to two things only: survival and the maintenance of the status quo. . . ."

Portal to E'ewere

MitY was already awake when the monitor inside her sleep cocoon began to vibrate. To stop the low humming before it could cause Offense to her baymates, she quickly turned it off, but she didn't climb down from her tier immediately, as she would have done on an ordinary day.

Still wrapped in her warm cocoon, she sat cross-legged on the sagging webbing of her bunk. She hadn't slept well; there was a throbbing deep inside her skull.

In the bunk beneath hers, Citizen virTue, who was a hydro-plant laborer on First Time, moaned softly in her sleep. The webbing of her bunk creaked noisily as she changed position. Far below, in the green-tinged shadows of the sleeping bay, most of the women who were on Second Time had already queued up at the sanitation stalls and the sonic-freshener booth, although a few stragglers were still climbing down from the upper reaches of the tiers.

Because the women of the bay were on separate time shifts, it was kept in perpetual semi-darkness, and there were only a few scattered safety lights to cast a green reflection over the women's pale bodies, the windowless walls and the cracked floor tiles.

Although the Courtesy Code forbade talking in the sleeping bays, it was never quiet here. There were always small rustling, coughs and sneezes and snores, the whisper of bare feet on tile, the hiss of air from the 'ditioners. The N'York/Bronx branch of the Sub-Trans System ran directly under the huge square building that housed AMitY's swarm. Every three minutes, one of its trains rocked through the underground tunnel, adding a deep-throated roar to the other noises of the bay.

Busy with her own thoughts, AMitY ignored the familiar sounds, the queues of shuffling women, the green-edged shadows. In an attempt to banish Discord from her thoughts, she bowed her head and folded her hands across her chest in the Stance for Meditation. But, as so often happened lately, Mind-Peace eluded her. Despite her training in the Disciplines, her thoughts kept straying to her own problems, and she couldn't help wondering what lay ahead for her today when she went before the Life Assignment Computer.

Life Computer Day. . . .

After all the years of grueling academic studies, the struggle to master the Disciplines, the endless Harmony and Order drills, the painful Peer Testings, Life-Comp Day was finally here.

A few hours from now, she would step up to the Assignment Computer and tap out the eleven letters and numbers of her Citizen's Identification Code on its shiny black keyboard. A few seconds later, she would know the pattern for the rest of her life—and she still hadn't achieved the Mind-Peace needed to accept the decision of the computer, no matter what it might be.

Let it be the Tenners. Oh, please—let the computer chose me for the Tenners today.

Inside her sleep cocoon, AMitY's skin prickled with a chill that had nothing to do with the clammy air of the bay. So much depended upon the decision of the Life Computer. Was she the only one in her class who had doubts, who found it strange that a citizen's future should be decided in the few seconds it took a slip of paper to be processed by the electronic circuits of a machine?

The pain started up behind her eyes again; she massaged her aching temples with her fingertips and told herself it was lack of sleep that made her head throb so. Even though she'd said the Litanies through from beginning to end, sleep had eluded her. Instead, she'd lain awake for hours, her mind returning again and again to the same old questions that had troubled her all her life:

Why am I so different from everybody else?

Why can't I achieve Harmony like other citizens?

Why do I have such unrealistic ambitions? Only one-tenth of my class can be chosen for advanced education—so why do I keep hoping that the computer will chose me, the daughter of Undesirables, for the Tenners?

And what's wrong with me that I want so desperately sometimes to be alone, out of sight and sound of other citizens? Are the ed-visors at school right when they say that those who fear closed-in places are throwbacks to pre-Chaos days? That it's an Atavism to crave solitude? What if they knew that sometimes I can hardly force myself to crawl into my sleep cocoon because I hate being shut in so much?

5

A slow trembling started up in AMitY's hands. The air around her seemed to thicken, and she was acutely aware now of the odor of unwashed sleep cocoons and the staleness of the inadequately conditioned air. As if the full weight of the swarm building, with its thousands of inhabitants, its hundreds of sleeping bays, its dozens of common rooms and corridors, service and energy units, were pressing down upon her, she felt as if she'd been caught in a vise that squeezed her chest and made it almost impossible to breathe.

Something else was wrong, too.

The walls of the bay seemed suddenly to dissolve away, letting in a golden light. AMitY gave an agonizing look downward. The door of the sonic-freshener had disappeared; an amber glow radiated through the opening, tinging the nude bodies of the waiting women with gold. Before she closed her eyes tightly, she caught a glimpse of something she knew was impossible—a lush valley, surrounded by jagged gray mountains. For a few seconds, until she put her hands over her ears, she heard singing, the sound of tinkling, bell-like voices.

A great yearning swelled up inside her. She wanted to reach out and embrace the light, to lose herself in its amber warmth. But reason told her it was a hallucination, that if she gave herself up to it, if she believed her eyes and ears and instincts, she would slip into insanity. So she fought against the seductive vision as she always did when it came, denying it, rationalizing it away. Slowly, the glow against her closed eyelids faded, and when she finally opened her eyes again to take another cautious look, the bay was shrouded in shadows again.

Drawing upon the Disciplines, she forced her body to relax, muscle by rigid muscle. When she had expurgated the last traces of the hallucination from her mind, she let the emptiness fill again, this time with the comforting words of the Litany for Living in Harmony:

I am one, one of many.
Each of us has his own Place of Being.
We live in Harmony.
I will not intrude upon the space of others;
They will not intrude upon my space.
I will not stare nor touch nor point
Nor raise my voice nor laugh aloud,
Lest I Offend.
I am one, one of many.
Each of us has his own Place of Being.
We live in Harmony.

Gradually, as the familiar words of the Litany spun through her mind, her breathing became normal. By the time she had finished, the panic had been banished. Even so, she said the Litany again before she slid out of her cocoon.

The air of the bay, kept at a chilly 10°C during the harsh N'York winters, curdled her nude body as she swung her legs over the bunk frame. As a non-status student and, at sixteen, one of the youngest women in the swarm, she only rated a top-level bunk in the swarm's noisiest—and most crowded—ménage. During the coming years, if she remained in Swarm 3-5254, she would move to progressively lower bunks in more favored ménages, graduating in time to one of the coveted top floor bays, eight stories above the street noise and the rumble of the Sub-Trans trains.

And then, when she was fifty-five, she would make a final move, this time to a ward in the Termination Swarms.

AMitY shivered convulsively. Always, when she thought of the Termination Swarms, an image of her grandfather rose before her, leaving her feeling cold and sick at heart.

She shook her head, repudiating her thoughts. Without further delay, she swung out onto the tier ladder and started down, her bare feet soundless on the icy rungs. From the top of a nearby tier, another pale figure was also descending. In the sallow light, AMitY recognized Citizen ModesTy, one of her classmates.

As she averted her eyes, courteously and allowed the other girl, who was a few days older and therefore her superior in status, to precede her into the sani-stalls, she wondered if, like her, Citizen ModesTy's sleep had been bothered by nightmares about the Life Assignment Computer.

When she came out of the sani-stalls, Citizen ModesTy had already passed into the sonic-freshener booth. Ignoring the bite of cold tile under her feet, AMitY assumed the Stance for Waiting—head bent, gaze downward, hands gripping her elbows. It was too bad, she thought idly, that the Code forbade friendship between baymates. Although she knew there was Harmony in the rule, it would have been comforting to share first-meal with Citizen ModesTy today and later to have a trek-mate during the hour-long trip to the Education Complex.

The green light above the freshener booth flashed on, signalling that Citizen ModesTy was finished and had moved into the locker room on the other side. AMitY stepped into the narrow enclosure and pressed the ON button. For the allotted fifty seconds, while the stream of sonic-agitated air cleansed her body, she luxuriated in the blessed warmth. Because this was one of the rare times when no one else was waiting for the booth, she pressed the ON button again and took an extra turn, even though she knew that it would earn her a black demerit if one of her baymates reported her to Citizen deCOrum, the ménage concierge.

Her skin still tingling from the friction of the agitated air, she opened the door of the bay locker room. Citizen ModesTy, already dressed in her student-blue robe, was standing by her locker braiding her long brown hair. Again, AMitY felt a pang of regret that it wasn't possible for them to be friends—or at least to exchange Comp Day greetings.

A tempting idea came to her. She hesitated, then gave a tiny shrug. After all, why not? In another three hours, they would achieve their new status; there was a good chance that both of them would be moving to separate ménages, perhaps to the Apprendice Swarms. And besides, who was to know? It was between shift-changes—and for the moment at least they were alone in the locker room.

The older girl straightened. AMitY took a step forward, smiling at her baymate. "A Harmon'ous Life 'Signment to you, Cit'zen ModesTy," she said softly.

But Citizen ModesTy didn't smile back. With a hiss of sucked-in air, she showed Offense. Hurriedly, she raised her cowl to hide her embarrassed face. A moment later, she had disappeared through the door that lead to the common rooms.

The reproof stung, even though AMitY knew she deserved it. Why was she always giving in to these impulses to reach out to other people, intruding upon their space? Hadn't she learned *anything* from the Disciplines?

The door opened to admit another woman. AMitY

turned away quickly and went to her own tiny locker to take out a neatly folded winter robe. Like Citizen ModesTy's, it was light blue, the color designating her status as a student. As she pulled it on, the coarse material, made of compressed sea-vegetation, rustled around her. Although it was the smallest adult size the ménage supply clerks had been able to come up with, it was still too long, and its hem brushed the floor when she bent to get her belt from the locker.

The belt, made of real leather, was very old, her only valuable possession. A family heirloom, passed down in her mother's family for generations, it had been given to her by her parents on the day she'd passed her Elevenses, the examination that assured her four additional years of academic studies. As she tied the strip of ancient leather around her narrow waist, she remembered the celebration that day. With her parents dead, her brother and grandfather living in separate swarms half a quadrant away, how different *this* day would be, no matter how Harmonious her Life Assignment might be.

AMitY's hands were unsteady as she hooked on her belt pouch and slipped the cord that held her Citizen's Identification Code tag over her head. Today, after she left the Education Complex, she would make the long trek to the Civic Complex to apply for a new tag. As she stared down at the familiar words on the square of laminated plastic now, she wondered soberly what changes in her status the new one would reflect.

CITIZEN IDENTIFICATION CODE: AM-5897-7688-Y (COMMON NAME: *AMitY*)
PLACE OF BEING: Bunk 54, Bay 3, Ménage

14, Swarm 5254, Quadrant 1, N'York City/ State, N'Eastern States of America
BIRTHDATE: 2 Ninth Month, Year 175 After Chaos
BIRTH PERMISSION CODE: MU-423-5790
SHIFT TIME: Second Time (Temporary: Student)
STATUS: Non-status (Temporary: Student)
SEXUAL PAIRING STATUS: ELIGIBLE
SEXUAL BONDING STATUS: ELIGIBLE (Provisional: See note below)
EUGENICS RATING: AAAA (Provisional: See note below)
(NOTE: Citizen's parents, now deceased, were Convicted Undesirables; see records of CH-9590-7354-H [CN: *CH*arity] and HB-9180-9800-F [CN: *H*armony])

AMitY touched the tag with her fingertip. Would she still be wearing the new one on a student-blue robe—or on the moss green of a medical technician? Or would she be issued the ugly olive-drab of a Sub-Trans worker? Was she fated to spend the rest of her life in the Subterranean Swarms? Working, eating, sleeping in the underground swarms, surfacing into the open air only twice a year for her ménage's annual Museum and Park Privilege Days?

She swallowed hard, fighting the sudden churning in her stomach. A passing woman gave her a covert glance, and she realized that while she'd been standing there, lost in thought, the locker room had gradually filled with stragglers from the First Time shift.

As the women brushed out their braids and un-dressed for baytime, AMitY was aware of their sliding, oblique glances. Part of their interest was because it bordered on a Courtesy lapse to linger in the locker room, once dressed, but some, she knew, stemmed from her unorthodox appearance.

She had long been aware that most of her ménage-mates suspected her of the Atavism of Vanity because of her vivid coloring, so different from the homologous paleness of most citizens. Although she'd never seen herself in a mirror, she'd been told that her eyes were an unusual green, that her facial skin, like the rest of her body was tawny, as if it had been kissed by the sun. So she was usually careful to keep her head covered, even in the locker room. Today, she'd been careless, and she sensed the thinly veiled disapproval of her baymates as she hurriedly raised her cowl.

But she forgot the women as soon as she'd turned her back on them. Although she shuffled toward the door at the proper speed, not too fast, not too slow, she moved to her own private Litany now.

Let the 'puter chose me for the Tenners . . . or if not that, at least let it be a 'signment above ground. Please don't let me be shut up in the darkness of the Sub-Swarms for the rest of my life. . . .

II

n the ménage canteen, AMitY queued up for a yeast wafer and a container of the nutritious but tasteless liquid called *firster*. She carried her food to a waiting wall in the main common room and slid sideways into an empty leaning rack. As she bowed her head and silently said the Litany for the Blessing of Firstmeal, she was grateful for the illusion of privacy the leaning rack afforded. Usually the bustle of the crowded common rooms was too familiar to bother her, but today she was acutely aware of the press of bodies, the closeness of the conditioned air, the insidious drone of whispering voices that seemed to set her bones to vibrating.

As she nibbled on the wafer and sipped the firster, she watched the newscaster screen on the opposite wall. Even though it was every citizen's duty to keep informed, she found it hard to concentrate on the moving ribbon of words. Somehow, it seemed unimportant today that plankton harvesting in the Seafarms was down for the third year in a row, that there'd been another accident in the Sub-Trans, that one of the older swarm buildings in Quadrant 4 had collapsed, or that an undetermined number of mauraders from the Outlands had been terminated by a squad of Barrier Guards during a raid on one of the O'Zone farms.

Too tense for hunger, AMitY lingered over her meal, idly watching the orderly lines of women shuffling past. In the canteen across from the waiting wall, some of the Third Time women were eating thirdmeal, the one sit-down meal of the day permitted ordinary citizens, while through the open door of the holovision room, three-dimensional figures flickered on the tiny holo-stage. Conversation was restricted to whispers here (and forbidden altogether in the holovision and meditation/reading rooms) but even so, a constant hum spilled out from the always-packed game room and from the energy room, where each citizen was expected to put in a weekly quota of hours at the energy wheels, replenishing the ménage batteries.

AMitY finished her firster, then joined the line at the nearest sonic-sterilizer. When her turn came, she dropped the empty container into the sterilizer, waited three seconds, then extracted it and put it away in her belt pouch. A few minutes later, as she queued up at the message counter, she had time to say the Fourth Litany through twice to prepare herself for disappointment before it was her turn to give her CIC number to the clerk.

She expected one message at the most, so when the woman laid four slips of transparent paper on the counter, she was so surprised that she almost lost Control and laughed out loud.

She carried the message slips into the mediation/reading room and was lucky enough to find an empty leaning booth. The first slip, a warm Comp Day greeting from her grandfather, was not unexpected, but the second, from her younger brother, was a complete surprise. Message slips cost two tokes—and HUmble's allotment as a Tenth Form student was not only minute, it was invariably in arrears because of his knack for collecting demerits.

The note, as breezy as HUmble himself, made AMitY smile, but she felt uneasy too as she read about her brother's latest Discipline Lapse, this time for an unauthorized chemistry experiment that had earned him a fine and twelve extra hours at his school's energy wheels.

AMitY folded the flimsy paper and made a mental note to talk to HUmble again about the folly of unbridled curiosity. Somehow she must impress upon him the importance of outward (if not inward) Discipline. No matter how high his intelligence rating, the son of Undesirables couldn't afford to show even one counter-Harmony trait, not if he wanted a decent Life Assignment someday.

She opened the third message slip. Her whole body stiffened as she read the brief message inside.

"Peace and Harmony, Citizen AMitY. Best wishes for a Harmonious Life Assignment today."

It was signed: "Citizen ConCord-Grissom."

AMitY's nostrils flared with disdain as she stared down at the Two-Name signature. With cold deliberation, she tore the note in tiny pieces and deposited them in a nearby trash receptacle.

The fourth note, from her best friend, which bubbled with optimism and humor, restored her smile. If PRudenCe had any secret doubts about the outcome of Comp Day for herself and AMitY, she hid them well.

"I've booked a privacy booth at the Ed-Complex

for half an hour," her letter ended. "Booth 23 at 0400 Second Time. I'm even furnishing tea-treat, so be there on time before it gets cold, Citizen Amble-Along-Deep-in-Thought."

AMitY read the slip again to make sure she hadn't misunderstood. A privacy booth for half an hour—and warm herbal tea from the vendor stalls, too! How could PRudenCe, on her student's allowance, possibly afford such a luxury? She puzzled over it a moment, then put it out of her mind, knowing the mystery would be solved when she saw her friend. She left the meditation room and headed for the nearest egress corridor, but before she reached it, a middle-aged woman, wearing the orange robe of a ménage concierge, stepped in front of her, blocking her way.

AMitY dipped her head in a respectful bow, but she didn't push back her cowl the prescribed inch, which would have been an invitation to exchange greetings. For one thing, she didn't want to be late; for another, Citizen deCOrum's company at any time was something to be avoided. Not only was she the ménage's concierge, she was its most notorious gossip, a Courtesy Code Zealot and the self-appointed guardian of Order for the whole swarm.

"I see you've been dawdl'n again, Cit'zen AMitY. Did you ov'sleep? Sloth is one of the Twenty Sins, you know." Citizen deCOrum's whisper was penetrating; inside her cowl, her coal-black eyes glittered with malice. "This is sure to cost you a black d'merit from your ed-visors!"

AMitY lowered her gaze, embarrassed by the woman's Courtesy Lapse. Only a reluctant pity stopped her from showing Offense with the customary hiss. Everybody in the ménage knew that Citizen deCOrum was almost fifty-five, that in another month or so she would be transferred to the Termination Swarms.

Despite the warmth of the crowded room, a shiver ran through AMitY's body. On Free-days, when she was permitted to visit her grandfather in the Termination Swarms, she always came away feeling grieved because there was so little she could do to relieve the crushing monotony of his life. Everything about the Termine wards repelled her—the dingy sleep cocoons and gray robes of the Termines; the rows of cots that overflowed into what had once been common rooms, so close-packed that visitors must either stand or else sit on the cots with their Termine host; the odor of aging bodies, an all-prevailing odor that the overworked 'ditioners couldn't quite dispel.

Most of all, she hated the miasma of despair that hung like a pall over the swarm, as much a part of the wards as the vacuous faces of the Termines. . . .

"Well, cit'zen? Swallow your tongue, have you?" Citizen deCOrum demanded.

"It's Life-Comp Day for my class," AMitY said, relenting. "I don't have to be at the Ed-Complex till 0400 Second Time."

Unexpectedly, the fluted lines of the woman's mouth softened. "So this is the day you go 'fore the 'signment 'puter, is it? Well, I'm not so termy that I can't 'member my own Comp Day. Like they say, it was 'flies in the stomach and hope in the heart.' I was so 'cited, I had to say the Good Lit'nies twice 'fore I could choke down firstmeal. But oh, I did draw a Harmon'ous 'signment, cit'zen! 'Mestic for a Two-Name family, the Paulsens, in one of the Museum Houses in Old Town, sit-down meals three times a day—and none of your yeast or synth-food wafers, either! No, it was all nat'ral food, fresh from the hydro-plants and O'Zone farms and Seafarms. Just three of us to a sleep 'cove, and bonus Park Day priv'leges every year. Yes, it was a good life, Cit'zen AMitY."

She paused to sigh, the lines of discontent deepening around her mouth. "Then my old mistress term'ated, and the new one 'cided she wanted younger 'mestics, so that was the end of it. I would've been sent to the Idle Swarms if my old master hadn't 'ranged this concierge 'signment for me. Well, like the Blessed Lit'nies say, we must all 'cept Order. Which doesn't mean a cit'zen can't hope for a Harmon'ous 'signment, does it? *You* could do a lot worse, a girl from the Common Swarms with Un'sirable parents, then a 'signment to Old Town as a 'mestic."

AMitY knew the concierge was right. Domestic service in Old Town was a highly coveted assignment for Common Swarm students. But since her own aspirations lay in another direction, she only nodded.

"I s'pose, like all young cit'zens these days, you have gran' ideas 'bout be'n a copto-pilot or maybe one of those holo'tainers?" Citizen deCOrum went on. "Well, high-stat 'signments don't go to students from the Commons. No matter what your ed-visors tell you, fam'ly c'nections are what count when the 'signments are handed out." She paused to evaluate the effect of her warning on AMitY. When AMitY maintained a polite silence, she added, "No matter what your 'signment, a pretty one like you will get plenty of court'n bids from the men, now that you've reached pair'n age. Just don't forget to pay proper 'tention to your work duties, Cit'zen AMitY. Pair'n mates come and pair'n mates go, but your Life Assignment is with you till the day you term'ate."

She pointed to the CIC tag dangling from AMitY's neck. "And don't count on that quad-A 'genics rat'n to get you out of the Commons. High-stat men who can 'ford private fam'ly ménages may bid for an hour in the pair'n units with a pretty swarm girl, but they pick one of their own status for perm'ent bond'n—"

She broke off to frown at a cluster of whispering women who had just left the holovision room. AMitY took advantage of the distraction to murmur a quick "Live in Harmony, cit'zen" before she headed for the egress corridor.

As she fell into line behind a woman wearing the dusty-pink robe of a midwife, she wondered what Citizen deCOrum would say about a swarm girl who dared hope that she would be chosen for the coveted Tenners so she could someday become a scientist like her grandfather had been.

And what would the concierge say if she ever found out that not only had AMitY, a girl from the Common Swarms, already received a permanent bonding bid from Citizen ConCord-Grissom, the son of an Old Town family, but that she'd been foolish enough to turn it down?

s AMitY shuffled along the egress corridor, she tried to put Citizen de-COrum's words out of her mind. She failed for the good reason that she knew the concierge spoke Truth. Students from the Common Swarms, no matter how promising, seldom were selected for anything higher than low-status assignments.

Unbidden, the old rebellion stirred. Before her parents' disgrace, her grades probably would have been high enough to earn her a place in the Tenners. But now she could only hope for some kind of miracle—and there were few miracles in a society ruled by Order.

It isn't fair, she thought. Just because her parents had spoken out in Public Forum against the new Eugenics Code, they had been stripped of status, labeled Undesirables, and sent to the Seafarms, which had proved to be a death sentence to both of them.

And it had been Chief Arbitrator conSistency-Grissom, one of the Council of Nine and ConCord-Grissom's father, who had passed the harshest sentence possible for their crime upon them. The case against her parents had been weak. After all, the Code did provide for Citizen Dissent. But there had been a rash of dissent over the new Eugenics Code, and her parents had been used as an example. Now they were dead, and she and HUmble lived half a quad apart and saw each other only on her Free-days. But Arbitrator conSistency-Grissom still lived with *his* family in Old Town, a respected member of the Council of Nine, the head authority of N'York State.

An indignant hiss brought AMitY back to the present. In her preoccupation, she had caused Offense by invading the space of one of her neighbors, a tall woman in porter-gray who was wearing a head rack heavily loaded with canteen supplies. AMitY ducked her head in apology and resolved to curb her wandering attention during the rest of the trek to the Education Complex.

The corridor, one of a dozen that served the swarm, was relatively quiet, but already she could hear the roar of the street up ahead. When she emerged from the swarm building a few minutes later, her ears were assaulted by a deep-throated hum, like a never-ending sigh.

The street sounds—sandals shuffling on cement; robes rustling; the inhaling and exhaling of breath; people whispering, sighing, coughing; all multiplied a thousandfold—were part of her life, something she seldom noticed. But today, as she shivered in the chill of the late fall air, her ears tingled unpleasantly, as if the sound had suddenly taken on a malignancy.

Although she banished the fancy from her mind, she had to apply special attention to the normally automatic task of passing through the slow outer lanes of traffic to the faster lanes inside the moving mass of people.

As she approached the corner of her own block-large swarm building and began the complicated maneuver of changing to one of the turning lanes, she passed a line of makeshift peddlers' stalls that huddled against the gray sides of the building.

Operated mostly by Idles and Undesirables, the stalls were tolerated by the Courtesy Guard as a harmless diversion and convenience for those swarm citizens who had the price of a dried fish cake, a sweet wafer, a container of warm herbal tea or, in summer, the mint-flavored concoction called a "cooler."

Some of the stalls dealt in more exotic items: handcrafted games small enough to fit into a citizen's belt pouch, a battered magazine or book that somehow had survived the years since commercial printing had been suspended; a strip of perfumed paper or a bit of bright ribbon for a courting woman; or, rarely these days, a handful of nuts or a few withered apples that had been smuggled in from the forbidden O'Zones.

AMitY ignored the wares displayed in front of each stall. Since she'd moved from the Family Swarms to the Commons, she'd seldom had the price of such luxuries, although she'd once saved her student's allotment for three months to buy a few tattered pages of a pre-Chaos history book for her grandfather's fifty-eighth birthday.

The street she turned into was one of the hundred arteries that crisscrossed the quadrant. Although wider than most, with its twelve lanes of foot traffic and its two lanes for the mo'carts of the Courtesy Guard and government officials, it was still so narrow that the swarm buildings that lined its sides kept it in perpetual shadow.

As AMitY drew close to the Education Complex,

she reversed the process she'd begun almost an hour earlier. Moving with practiced ease, she slid into empty spaces as they opened up around her, ending up in the outside lane again. Ahead, she saw the cluster of privacy booths that serviced the Education Complex; a few minutes later, she was standing in front of Booth 23.

Despite its name, the booth offered very little real privacy. The lower half, constructed from the same gray apoxy-concrete as the swarm buildings, was only waist high. The resinglas upper half, although tinted a smoky gray, wasn't opaque enough to completely shield the occupants from the eyes of passersby, and the partitions between the booths were so thin that whispers were the only prudent way to guard against eavesdroppers.

Even so, the booths were very popular with couples in the preliminary stages of pairing; for private trading, a practice called "swaphopping"; and for the exchange of family news too sensitive for the crowded common rooms.

PRudenCe must have been watching for her because the entrance panel slid open even before AMitY had time to tap for admittance.

"Peace and Gluttony, Cit'zen Amble-Along." PRudenCe's dark eyes danced as she pressed a container of lukewarm tea into AMitY's hand. At AMitY's involuntary laugh, her friend looked shocked and gave a hiss of mock-Offense, making AMitY laugh even harder.

Although the herbal tea was weak and only slightly sweet, she sipped the rare treat gratefully. Trust PRudenCe to find a way to make Comp Day, with all its terrors, seem like a celebration. And how in Harmony had she been lucky enough to find such a friend just when she needed one so badly? If she hadn't met PRudenCe that first day in the new school, how lonely this past year would have been!

She'd still been in shock from grief when she'd reported to the new school in the Common Swarms that day. She'd felt totally out of Harmony with her new classmates, who'd eyed her coldly and whispered busily to each other behind their hands. Then the dark-skinned girl sitting on the next mat in the Place of Assembly had smiled at her, and as she'd returned the smile, somehow she had known that she would have at least one friend at her new school.

And now, a year later, they would be going their separate ways again. Even if they were both assigned to the same Apprendice Swarm, it would be only for a short time. In two months, when PRudenCe turned sixteen, she would be segregated in the Sterie Swarms, forbidden to associate with anyone not a Sterie like herself.

PRudenCe's smile faded, and AMitY knew that her intuitive friend had sensed her pain and had guessed its cause.

But PRudenCe came up with another smile, albeit a wobbly one. "So today we go 'fore the all-powerful Life 'Signment 'Puter," she said lightly. "And in a few months, it's me for the merry life of a Sterie, hi ho."

AMitY winced at the determined cheerfulness in her friend's voice. Since the harsh new Eugenic Code had taken effect a year ago, PRudenCe had known that when she came of age at sixteen, she would be sterilized. One of her ancestors, six generations back, had been a borderline diabetic, and although the malady hadn't manifested itself in any of her descendants since, it was enough to deprive PRudenCe of her right to bear a child, to forbid her from bonding permanently (or even from a temporary pairing) with anyone not a Sterie like herself.

It also meant that her citizen's right to the Universal Panacea would be curtailed—and everybody knew that life without the wonder enzyme that stimulated the body's defenses against disease was apt to be short.

"It's a stupid law," AMitY burst out, forgetting the thinness of the walls. At PRudenCe's worried glance toward the two middle-aged men in the next booth, she lowered her voice to an impassioned whisper. "My grandfather says that if a genetic disorder doesn't show up in six gen'rations, the d'fective gene has bred out or, mo' likely, it wasn't diagnosed right in the first place. The Code Board is just try'n to find new ways to 'strict the birthrate and d'prive cit'zens of their right to the Panacea. It just isn't fair to keep you and Cit'zen UNison from bond'n!"

PRudenCe's eyes clouded, and AMitY was sorry she'd mentioned UNison. Since childhood, her friend and Citizen UNison had been committed to each other. Until the passage of the new Eugenics Code, they'd had no reason to doubt that someday they would be granted permission to bond.

"Careful—your bias is show'n, Cit'zen Loyalty," PRudenCe said. "And it isn't all that bad. I hear Steries lead ding-dong lives—no 'spons'bil'ties, no worries 'bout status. Who knows? Maybe I'll catch the eye of some termy old hi'stat, and he'll set me up in a pleasure unit in the Artisan Swarms and feed me nat'ral food three times a day."

"Don't you *dare* joke about someth'n like that," AMitY said crossly.

It was well known that some of the younger Sterie women were exploited by high-status men, those powerful enough to arrange for private pleasure units. And PRudenCe, with her glossy black hair, her lustrous dark eyes and radiant smile was so very lovely. . . .

"Oh, PRudenCe," she burst out. "If there was only someth'n you could do 'fore—"

"Shhh . . . those two swaphoppers in the next booth will hear you and 'port you for spread'n Dissent. And 'sides,"—PRudenCe smiled suddenly—"it will all work out. We're three-cappers, aren't we? And ev'body knows that three-cappers are lucky."

Despite herself, AMitY had to smile. That first day, when they'd exchanged names and histories during secondmeal, they'd made the discovery that both of them had three-capital names. It was so rare that all three of a citizen's CIC letters could be utilized in one of the authorized common names that PRudenCe and AMitY had decided on the spot that they were special and destined to be lifelong friends.

Although they had other similarities, they seldom talked about those. Both were orphans, both were the daughters of convicted Undesirables—and both had siblings, more and more uncommon as the Eugenics Code became increasingly strict. Even twelve years earlier, it had been only the rare quad-A eugenics rating of both AMitY's parents plus their status as government administrators that had permitted them a second child—and then only because their first had been a girl.

But PRudenCe's sister, four years her junior, was an Illegal. Because the child wasn't entitled to an official Citizen's Identification Code, her mother had given her the common name of Tutu, borrowing the first two digits of her own CIC.

That Tutu had been born at all was an accident. Her mother, who had just lost her bond-mate in a Sub-Trans accident, had made the dangerous decision not to report her pregnancy to the Birth Board and submit to an abortion.

Somehow, she had managed to conceal her condition under her all-encompassing robe, and after the baby was born (on a Free-day in the privacy of the sleeping alcove she shared with PRudenCe) she used her position as a midwife to hide the baby in an Idle Swarms nursery, using false papers.

Eventually, a routine audit revealed her crime. She was convicted of Gross Insult to the Code, and because of the severity of her crime, her life was terminated. Tutu, then three, was banished to a school for Illegal children. There she was receiving a limited education, mainly in the Disciplines. At sixteen, she too would be sterilized and would live out her life in the Sterie Swarms. . . .

"Will you be able to visit Tutu after you are—after your sixteenth birthday?" AMitY asked PRudenCe now.

"I doubt it. Steries aren't p'mitted to go into the Idles, you know. 'Course, we could be 'signed to the same swarm someday." Although she smiled, the bleakness in PRudenCe's eyes belied her optimistic words. "How's HUmble? Still c'lect'n black d'merits right and left?"

AMitY sighed. "He had 'nother Reprimand from his ed-counselor last week—"

As she went on to recount HUmble's latest escapade, she couldn't help a secret relief that at least HUmble had a chance for a better life than that of a Sterie's—or as a drone in the Idles. Wasn't there a childs' tale about a boy from the Common Swarms who had risen as high as the Citizens' Council? Of course, even if it wasn't just a legend, it must have happened a long time ago. These days, everything conspired to keep a citizen in the same status as his parents, often with the same Life Assignment.

It was the children of Two-Name families, the descendants of the original Council of Nine, who received elite assignments as Government officials, farm managers, holo-tainers and copto-pilots. The children of high-status parents became the professionals, the chief administrators, the scientists and ed-visors. Only to the most promising Common Swarm student was even a mid-status assignment possible.

And seats on the Council of Nine, the highest authority in the state, were hereditary. Someday ConCord-Grissom would take his father's place on the Council. ConCord's children—he would be permitted two if his first one was a girl—would receive privileges denied most citizens, even those of high status. As long as one male Grissom remained, he and his family would occupy Grissom Museum House, immune to the irritants and stresses that common citizens faced every second of their lives.

So why had she refused ConCord's bonding bid? What had she really proved by turning him down? Even now, it might not be too late. She could send a message slip to ConCord saying she'd changed her mind, and then she too could live in Old Town, enjoy a fulfilling Life Assignment, be permitted at least one child. The Grissom patronage would surely extend to her brother, assuring HUmble a place on the Tenners and a decent Life Assignment someday that would utilize that busy, inquisitive mind of his. Just because she hated ConCord's father for what he'd done to her parents, did she have the right to deny HUmble his one chance to escape from the Commons?

"Don't look so glum," PRudenCe said. " 'Member, Cit'zen Rebellion—'Each of us in his own Place of Being, Equal under the Code,' even if"—she smiled wickedly—"some are more equal than others."

But this time, AMitY didn't laugh at her friend's irreverence. "Yes, some *are* more equal than others, and they make the laws. If only there was a way out for people like you and Tutu, a place where you would be safe from the Eugenic Code."

"Where?" PRudenCe, always practical, asked. "Private cit'zens can't travel outside their own quad these days, not without p'mission passes. 'Sides, ev'ry place is the same, at least 'hind the Barriers, and who wants to live in the Outlands? It's a jungle out there. No Order, no Court'sy Code—"

"There's always the O'Zones," AMitY said in a low voice.

PRudenCe shook her head. "Even if we could get past the gates, 'ventually the rangers would find us and then we'd be worse off then 'fore. We'd be—" She broke off, a pinched look around her nostrils.

You'd be sent to the Seafarms to die like my parents did, AMitY finished silently. The punishment for trespassing in the Oxygen Zones, those precious strips of land between quadrants that were allowed to go wild because the oxygen they replenished was so desperately needed in the crowded city/states, was banishment to the Seafarms.

And citizens sent to harvest plankton in the Seafarms could expect short lives. Even if they survived the dangerous depths of the plankton fields for a little while, they soon lost their ability to live at sea level and were doomed to spend the rest of their lives in the pressurized domes of the Sea Swarms.

"I know you're right," AMitY said aloud. "But I still can't help think'n there must be someth'n better for you and Tutu, for all of us."

"You're a dreamer, AMitY." PRudenCe studied her with narrowed eyes. "And speak'n of dreams—have you had that one about be'n in the O'Zones lately?"

AMitY hesitated; what would PRudenCe think if she told her the truth, that the dreams had become something more in the past few months?

"Sometimes—only it isn't really the O'Zones," she said, deciding on a half-truth. "The light is like—well, like liquid gold. Some of the trees are strange, too, unlike anyth'n I've ever seen at the State Arbor'um or on the holo, but—oh, it's so beau'ful there, PRudenCe! My dream is always the same. I'm 'lone and I'm run'n—can you 'magine be'n able to run as fast as you like? The only sound is the wind, and ev'th'n smells so fresh and sweet—like the p'fumed paper the peddlers sell to court'n women. And it all seems so real. Sometimes, ev' after I 'waken, I can still smell the flowers."

She stopped, ashamed of the raw yearning in her voice.

"Well, it sounds ding-dong, but I think I'd be 'fraid, be'n 'lone like that," PRudenCe confessed. "I'm not as brave as you—and 'sides, my dreams are dif'rent. I always dream 'bout—"

She broke off, flushing. AMitY suppressed a smile because she knew that PRudenCe's dreams were about UNison.

"I guess we do dream 'bout famil'ar th'ns," PRu-denCe went on. "After all, I've never been 'lone 'cept in the 'freshner—and then I can *hear* other people. But you were 'lone that time in the O'Zones. Maybe that's why you keep hav'n the same dream."

"The dreams started long 'fore that. I've had them all my life. I'm run'n down a wooded hillside and through the trees, I can see—" She broke off, suddenly reluctant to share that experience, the fleeting glimpses she'd had of something wonderful and strange.

"Weren't you 'fraid that time in the O'Zones?"

"No—oh, I was worried 'bout HUmble, but—no, I wasn't 'fraid. It felt nat'ral, as if I b'longed there."

"And that's the day you met Cit'zen ConCord-Grissom for the first time, wasn't it? Oh, it's so r'mantic! Just like one of those holo-plays 'bout the old days."

"Well, it wasn't like that," AMitY said dryly. "I was only fifteen and ConCord was 'most twenty. He thought me still a child. So it wasn't ver' r'mantic at all—"

But it had been something much better, of course. It had been a day of pure magic, AMitY thought silently, and suddenly she was confronted with a flood of memories of that day, the one that had irrevocably closed her childhood, separating her life into two sections: before and after her meeting with ConCord-Grissom. . . .

I V

AMitY had turned fifteen just two months before she met ConCord for the first time. It was her family's Park Privilege Day, a twice-yearly outing to which her parents' duel assignments as mid-status government administrators entitled the family.

Although AMitY knew that other citizens were more and more opting for authorized substitutes for their annual Park Day, for once she was glad that her parents observed the old ways religiously and still considered Park Day a tradition, if not a duty.

The Parkland to which they'd been assigned was a strip of land covered with patchy grass that adjoined one of the quadrant's Oxygen Zones. By the time they arrived, it was already filling with other Second Time picnickers. They threaded their way along the narrow paths that separated the plots and unfolded their seagrass mats on the small strip of grass assigned to them for the next eight hours. Leaving HUmble, who was eleven, in AMitY's care, her parents went off to draw picnic rations at the Park Canteen.

Although Citizen Harmony, AMitY's father, had

grumbled under his breath about the location of the plot (the favored ones were in the center, close to the sanitation booths and the Canteen) AMitY was secretly delighted with the one they'd drawn because it was bordered on one side by the O'Zones's thicket barriers, which gave them more privacy.

As soon as her parents were out of sight, AMitY flung back her cowl to let the sun's rays warm her skin, ignoring the disapproving glances from the family and ménage groups nearby.

When she saw that HUmble was engrossed in the study of an ant hill, she stretched out on her mat. With her eyes closed against the unaccustomed brightness, with the wind stirring the tendrils of hair that had escaped her braids, it was almost possible to believe she was alone. Only the murmur of voices and the rustle of robes reminded her that it was just an illusion.

She drifted into half-consciousness, her thoughts without form. Maybe she fell asleep, because when she opened her eyes again, a few minutes later, there seemed to be a golden haze, like the residue from one of her dreams, over the milling groups around her. The haze disappeared when she bit down hard on her tongue. Automatically, she looked around for HUmble, only to discover that he was gone.

She'd had no way of knowing then that he'd wandered off in the wake of a sweet ice vendor or that he would wander back a few minutes later, having spent a month's allowance on a container of crushed ice and a few drops of syrup. She only knew that her brother, with his insatiable curiosity and his penchant for getting into trouble, was gone—and that her parents had left HUmble in her care.

Even now, two years later, she could still remember how her heart had raced as she'd stared around frantically, not caring if she caused Offense.

Although it was a Lapse of Courtesy to speak to any citizen in the Parklands who was not from one's own group, AMitY had just gotten up the courage to ask a nearby woman if she'd noticed a small boy with red hair go by, when she noticed what seemed to be a fresh break in the thick growth of the O'Zone barrier.

As she stared at the small round opening in the thicket, all the stories she'd ever heard about lost children who'd been devoured by the wild animals rumored to roam the O'Zones went through her mind. A more realistic fear was her knowledge that even HUmble's youth and her parents' status couldn't save him from the Seafarms if the rangers discovered him in the forbidden O'Zones. A smaller but still potent worry was the realization that blame for any trouble HUmble, the boy of the family, might get into was sure to be placed squarely upon her shoulders by her parents.

So she waited until her nearest neighbors, a hemp weavers' Guild group from the Artisan Swarms, were gathered in a tight privacy circle while they ate their picnic rations before she wriggled into the small break in the thicket.

The belt of untrimmed shrubbery was in full leaf, so dense that it was only by pure chance that the opening she'd found went all the way through to the other side. At first, she looked for HUmble frantically, not really taking in her surroundings. Afraid to call his name for fear a ranger might hear her, she searched through clumps of undergrowth and looked behind nearby trees.

She was passing a small shrub when she saw the

butterfly. It was clinging to a twig, its still-wet wings quivering spasmodically. A feeling of familiarity, as if she'd experienced this moment before, drove everything else from her mind. She watched with entranced eyes as it rose in a flurry of purple-and-gold wings. It swirled in circles above her head, and something—a magic, a delirium of the senses—took over. Suddenly she was aware that, for the first time in her life, she was completely alone, out of sight of any other human being.

Later, she would be ashamed that she forgot HUmble in that first rush of joy. All that mattered was the novelty of standing alone beneath a sky that was empty of everything man-made, with the sun warming her skin, with the rich odor of earth and growing things in her nostrils, with the wind, fresh and unsullied by the pollution of methane units or swarm building exhaust fumes, pushing against her face and whipping her robe against her legs.

The wind caught the wings of the butterfly; it swerved erratically, then regained its balance and took off, skimming the tops of the trees. AMitY followed it. As if she'd just discovered the use of her legs, she ran through the woods, across a narrow strip of meadow, down a small hill, the butterfly a purple-and-gold beacon before her.

For the next few minutes, in her mindless plunge through the woods, all caution was suspended. Even after the butterfly disappeared, she kept on running with shameless abandon, her cowl flung back, her head high, intoxicated by the certainty that she had finally found her true Place of Being.

When her legs, unaccustomed to such strenuous activity, finally gave out, she dropped down on a fallen log to rest. For a while, she watched a small, brown animal—a squirrel? a chipmunk?—busily eating a nut under a tree. It was only later that she would marvel at her lack of fear at seeing, for the first time in her life, an animal that wasn't penned up in a cage at the Quadrant Menagerie.

When the animal finally took alarm and darted away, she rose and followed it. It quickly disappeared behind a tree, but by then, she had found the brook.

For a long time, she stood there on a grassy bank, staring down at the swirling, tumbling water, at the gray rocks, wet with spray. She'd never seen open fresh water before, and it drew her, tempted her as if it were a magnet and she a bit of metal. For a while, she resisted its pull—and then she kicked off her sandals and eased into the bubbling water, holding up the hem of her robe with her hands to keep it from getting wet.

When she realized the cumbersome robe was limiting her movements, she stripped it off and tossed it up on the bank beside her sandals. She waded out until the water reached her waist, and again it seemed to her that she was reliving something she'd done before, that the only thing missing was the pervasive golden light to make this the place of her dreams.

How long she stayed there, splashing herself and playing with a floating leaf, she was never sure. When she made the exciting discovery that the buoyancy of the water would hold her up, she floated on her back, not caring that the water was washing over her face and drenching her braids. Everything—HUmble's disappearance, her own danger—faded into unimportance in the sheer tactile delight of the moment.

And then she heard a sound behind her, and when she looked up, a tall, dark-haired man was watching her from the bank.

Like a blow to the stomach, the magic vanished, replaced by fear, by a realization of the enormity of her crime.

For a long moment, she stared at the stranger. He wore the forest green robe of an O'Zone Ranger; his cowl was pushed back, and despite her fear, she noticed the strength of his features, the glossiness of his brown facial hair. From the fullness of his beard and the length of his hair, she knew he had not yet reached twenty-one, the age when, by custom, male citizens trimmed their hair to a shorter length.

She was wondering why he was so silent, when he turned his back abruptly. "You'd better get out of the water and put on your robe 'fore you turn blue, cit'zen," he said gruffly.

Only AMitY's pride, an Atavism that all her training in the Disciplines hadn't been able to cure, kept her from bursting into tears and bawling like a baby. With as much dignity as she could summon, she climbed out of the water. Silently she pulled on her robe, slipped her narrow feet back into her sandals and fastened her belt around her waist.

As if he sensed when she had finished dressing, the man turned, and she saw he was smiling. Even before he spoke, the same instinct that had kept her from raising her cowl, told her that she was in no danger from this stranger with his wide, humorous mouth and his warm brown eyes.

"You'd better dry your hair 'fore I take you back to the Parklands," he said matter-of-factly. "If we meet a Parkie, wet hair might be hard to 'splain on a sunny day like this."

Shyly, AMitY nodded. When he dropped down on a patch of grass, she joined him, choosing a spot a few feet away. Although he watched her openly, she didn't take Offense as she unwound her loosened braids and tossed her hair with both hands, letting the wind dry the thick, coppery strands.

"How old are you, cit'zen?" he asked abruptly.

"Fifteen. My name is AMitY," she said, then added the customary, "Capital AM and Y."

He was silent for a moment. "I s'pose your parents call you AMY in the priv'cy of your own ménage?"

"Oh, no. They're ver' orth'dox." She ducked her head to hide a smile. "But my brother calls me all sorts of th'n's when he can get 'way with it."

He threw his head back in a laugh, and AMitY stared at the strong column of his throat, suddenly uneasy again. What she had assumed was the natural brownness of his skin, she now realized, was a deep tan. What kind of citizen would deliberately expose his face to the sun long enough to get such a tan? Did this man belong to one of those odd cults who stole up to the roofs in the Artisan Swarms to sunbathe without their robes? Was this why he seemed so unconcerned about her own criminal behavior?

"I've never seen hair that color 'fore," he said. "It's like burnished copper."

Although she wasn't sure what he meant, she knew it must be a compliment. She ducked her head again, this time to hide the warmth that rose to her cheeks. "It runs in my mother's fam'ly," she said. "My grandfather has the same color of hair and so does HUmble—"

She broke off as consternation hit her. It was only then, speaking HUmble's name aloud, that she remembered why she was here.

The man frowned. "Are you 'fraid I'll 'port you? I won't, you know. The Code is much too harsh on

O'Zone 'truders. Maybe at one time the penalty was needed to keep cit'zens from ov'run'n the Zone, but no one comes here these days 'cept rangers. You're the first 'truder I've ever come 'cross. Don't be 'fraid I'll turn you in, Cit'zen AMitY."

"It isn't that. It's my brother. I came here look'n for him—" As she went on, pouring out her fears for HUmble's safety, the man listened intently, and she wondered why it was so easy to confide in this stranger, while it was so difficult to talk to her own parents. What would her father say, for instance, if he knew she was using familar speech to an O'Zone ranger instead of the formal language his status warranted?

"Don't worry, Cit'zen AMitY," the man said when she finally ran down. "I'll help you find your brother. If he's already been d'tained by 'nother ranger, I'll see that he's turned over to your parents with just a Reprimand."

"You can do *that,* Cit'zen Ranger?" AMitY asked.

He hesitated, then said with obvious reluctance, "My name is ConCord-Gissom. My father is Chief Arb'trator conSistency-Grissom."

AMitY already knew he must be from a high status family. Only the sons of such families were allowed the privilege of serving four years with the O'Zone rangers. But a Two-Namer, the son of the Chief Arbitrator—she shrank away, knowing she must look as frightened as she felt.

"I won't bite," he said with a grimace. "I'm made of the same stuff as other cit'zens."

AMitY gave him a doubtful look. He sounded— yes, almost defensive, as if he were used to other citizens being uncomfortable in his presence.

"I know that," she said impulsively. "I won't hold

your status 'gainst you, Cit'zen ConCord-Grissom."

His laugh startled her, but he sobered quickly. "You're a rarity these days, Cit'zen AMitY, Capitol AM and Y. I have a feel'n we're go'n to be friends."

Suddenly, as quickly as it had vanished, the magic was back. AMitY found herself answering ConCord questions about her parents, her brother, her school as if he were someone from her ménage group that she'd known all her life. She told him about her ambition to be a scientist like her grandfather ausTere, about her grief when he'd reached Termination age the year before and had been transferred to the Termine Swarms.

And then, as if ConCord's eyes had some mesmerizing power, she told him about the dreams of the strange golden world that had haunted her most of her life. It was only when she found herself confiding that sometimes, in the past couple of years, the dream had come to her during waking hours, that she stopped, realizing how dangerous such an admission could be.

But ConCord didn't look Offended. "I have my dreams, too," he told her. "Someday I mean to change this world of ours, to find a way out of the trap we've fallen into."

A wordless protest rose to AMitY's lips. To speak such things aloud—and to a stranger—was reckless. Did the son of the Chief Arbitrator think he was immune to the Code?

"Surely you've had such thoughts yourself?" he asked, and she knew that he'd caught her dismay.

AMitY hesitated, then said cautiously, "I *have* wished there were more Parklands so ev'ry cit'zen could be 'lone once in a while."

"I doubt many would take advan'age of the

op'tun'ty. We're a nation of agoraphobics these days. It's even b'com'n dif'cult to get 'cruits for the rangers. 'Course there's always plenty of vol'teers for the Court'sy Guard."

"There must be thousands of mid-status cit'zens eager for the chance to be a Park or O'Zone Ranger. Why not open the 'signments to them?"

ConCord shrugged. "The Council is 'fraid it would sow Dissent and upset the Status Quo. So we struggle 'long with the few rangers we have. Right now, the O'Zones are so poorly p'trolled that a cit'zen could stay hidden here for weeks. Which is why the tales of wild an'mals are circ'lated." He gave her a curious look. "Weren't you 'fraid you'd meet up with a rav'nous tiger, Cit'zen AMitY?"

"It never 'curred to me," she confessed.

"Well, that fear keeps out the more adven'rous— the few that are left. Most cit'zens are uneasy even in the Parklands these days. That's why so many of them chose alt'nate priv'leges to their Park Days."

AMitY digested his words in silence. She was suddenly remembering how cross her father had been because their alloted plot was on the perimeter of the Parklands instead of in the crowded middle. "I'm even more dif'rent than I thought," she said soberly. " 'Cause I'd give up my birthright to the Panacea for a tour as a ranger."

She stared around at the trees, at the sunlight dancing off the waters of the brook. "How will you bear to leave all this"—she gestured at the brook—"when your tour of duty is up?"

"It isn't as bad for me as it is for other cit'zens," ConCord told her. "Old Town, where I live, is more comfortable than the Swarms. And I'll be busy, too, when I take my father's place on the Council, three years from now. I hope to find solutions to our problems, not just new ways to maintain the Status Quo. The life of ev'ry cit'zen should be rich and full, not just the lives of a priv'leged few. There should be space and fresh air and nat'ral food for all—"

"But how is that pos'ble? There isn't enough space for that."

"There's plenty of room—beyond the Barriers."

A chill ran through AMitY. Unconsciously, she lowered her voice to a whisper. "You mean the Outlands? But ev'body knows the Outlands are ruled by savages."

"In the old days, yes. But nobody's been beyond the Barriers, not even the Sea Barriers, for a gen'ration. The last time a squad of Barrier Guards went into the Outlands, look'n for a partic'larly pesky band of mauraders, they found only a few wand'r'n tribes, no wild an'mals, no monsters—noth'n but empty land. Their 'ports were s'pressed, but I b'lieve they spoke Truth."

"Then why were their 'ports s'pressed?"

Again, he gave an impatient shrug. "Like most Councils, that one didn't want to open the gates to change. Sev'ral of the Arb'trators on the present Council—my father is not one of them—are less c'serv'tive than normal, but even they would have to see more proof than a couple of outdated reports 'fore they'd take any action. I hope to change all that when I take my father's place on the Council."

"What will you do?" AMitY asked, fascinated by the determination in his voice.

"I'll take a group of hearty cit'zens into the Outlands to 'splore and bring back ev'dence that our fears have blinded us, that for decades, maybe even longer, we've ov'est'mated the dangers out there."

"But what 'bout mauraders?" she protested. "The newscaster 'ports their raids all the time."

"There are a few wild tribes, yes. But they stay 'way from the Barriers. The ones we've had trouble with are ren'gades, outcasts."

"Have you ever seen one?"

"Several times. I even talked to one 'fore he was ter'mated. He looked much like we do—under a few layers of dirt. Our language was 'nough 'like that we un'stood each other." He smiled grimly. "He said we were devils, that it was only when hunt'n was poor and they were starv'n that they'd risk capture by raid'n our fields. When I asked why his people didn't raise their own crops, he looked shocked, said farm'n was the Devil's way. I 'spect it's some kind of r'ligion, a cult that lives off the land. Which is 'nother reason to 'lieve there are few people out there."

AMitY studied the eagerness in his eyes, and suddenly she was afire with an idea. "I want to go with you," she blurted. "And my grandfather, too. He's a biol'gist, and sometimes he talks like you. Once, just 'fore he was sent to the Termine Swarms, he told me he had doubts 'bout an Order that teaches equal'ty and d'mands so much from most of its cit'zens while at the same time, it b'stows priv'leges on a few simply 'cause they were born into the right—" She stopped, her hand flying up to cover her mouth, appalled at her own loose tongue.

But ConCord was smiling again. "That 'splains someth'n that puzzled me 'bout you. Somehow, you don't seem to match what you've told me 'bout your parents. I think I'd like to meet Cit'zen ausTere."

4 3

His eyes held a strange intensity that made AMitY aware of their close proximity on the grassy mound, of her exposed head. Hastily, she began braiding her hair, her eyelids lowered.

"And it's time I took you back to your parents," ConCord said. He rose, pulling his cowl over his head. He waited silently until she had finished with her hair and was adjusting her own cowl before he asked, "If I ask your father for 'mission to visit you in your fam'ly ménage, would you 'ject?"

AMitY found she'd lost her voice. She shook her head, sensing that her life had just taken a new turn, that her meeting with the stranger would have far-reaching consequences to her future.

The next day, a formal invitation arrived, inviting AMitY and her family, as well as the other five families of their ménage, to tour Grissom Museum House as the guests of Citizen ConCord-Grissom.

Although AMitY, at fifteen, was aware of the vast gulf that separated a mid-stat girl from the son of the State's Chief Arbitrator, she was surprised at the excitement the invitation caused. When her father, his expression even more stern than usual, took her aside, she was very careful to hide her elation.

"I don't un'stand how this honor could fall 'pon such an unDis'plined girl, but it seems you've caught the fancy of Cit'zen ConCord-Grissom. It's ver' un-Orth'dox. Cit'zens should stay in their own status." He gave her a sharp look. "I 'spect you to 'serve all the Court'sies, AMitY. No 'schang'n bold looks, no touch'n hands, no laugh'n out loud with Cit'zen ConCord-Grissom. There'll be no loose b'havior in *my* family."

And AMitY had nodded meekly, her eyes demure.

Three days later, ConCord himself escorted the awed group through the four-hundred-old Old Town house, showing them its marvels of natural woods and metals and bricks, its antique furnishings, its priceless collections of centuries-old plastics and kitchen utensils, some so oddly shaped, like a long tube of wood with handles on each end, that their exact use was no longer known.

In the public rooms, he pointed out a photograph, encased in plastic, of the Grissom who had founded their family and explained that his ancestor had represented the military on the first Council of Nine. As AMitY studied the unbearded man in the photograph, she wondered if ConCord were a throwback to his ancestor—and then wondered why the thought, instead of repelling her, only made her want to know him better.

Later, as ConCord passed around a tray of sweet wafers and containers of tea, observing Courtesy by offering the treats in strict order of his guests' ages, only AMitY seemed to notice the glint of humor in his deep-set eyes.

They were leaving to return to their ménage when he drew her father aside and asked if he might make courtship calls upon AMitY. Somehow, she wasn't surprised that her father, after only the smallest hesitation, granted his permission.

ConCord's visits, in the crowded common room her family shared with the other families of their ménage, were brief, formal, very correct. Always, he brought with him a gift of sweet wafers or dried fruit or soy-tein bars, enough to be shared with the rest of the ménage so as not to arouse the Harmony Lapse of

Envy. Discreetly, he arranged for a few outings for the whole ménage—a visit to the Quadrant Menagerie to see a touring field-and-woods animal exhibit, a seldom-permitted tour of an O'Zone farm.

Although it would have been a breach of Courtesy to comment openly on ConCord's interest in AMitY, she knew she was the object of gossip from the oblique looks, the deference paid to her not only by ménage-mates her own age, but by the adults of the ménage. Even the attitude of her father, always the disciplinarian, had mellowed now that he'd permitted ConCord's attentions to his daughter.

It was taken for granted by everyone that when AMitY turned sixteen, her father would grant Citizen ConCord-Grissom first pairing privileges. Only AMitY knew that it would be something more, that ConCord meant to ask for permanent bonding with her.

Since private conversation was difficult in the crowded common room, she never knew for sure what ConCord's parents thought of his interest in a mid-stat girl, although she realized that the special privileges could only have come through his father. And the whole question became irrelevant when, a month before her sixteenth birthday, her parents were charged with Gross Insult to Order, declared Undesirables, and sent to the Seafarms. Before AMitY had time to adjust to the separation from her family, both of them were dead, killed by the dangerous depths of the plankton fields.

And it was ConCord's father, Chief Arbitrator conSistency-Grissom, who had sent them there to die.

In her first grief and anger, she had vowed never to speak to ConCord again, to refuse even the smallest favor from him. In the year since, she had broken that vow just once, and that only because he had arranged for HUmble to be quartered in an Artisan Swarm school. She had refused the same favor for herself, even though the alternative was a sleeping bay in the Common Swarms; and when he sent her messages, she torn them up, refusing his invitations, his request for a meeting.

It only exacerbated her anger when, on her sixteenth birthday, he put in a Permanent Bonding bid with her, after all. Across the face of the official form, she scrawled a line of black X's and sent it back.

And I'm not sorry I did it, AMitY told herself now.

Beside her, PRudenCe finished off the last of her tea-treat with a contented sigh. AMitY, realizing that she'd been wasting precious time with her brooding, smiled at her friend.

"Thank you for the tea-treat and the Comp Day message, PRudenCe," she said. "I wanted to send you one, too, but—"

"—but you spent all your tokes this month pay'n off HUmble's fines. And you're won'r'n how I can 'ford booth time, aren't you? As it happens, it was a Comp Day gift from a friend."

Before AMitY could ask if Citizen UNison was her generous friend, there was a tapping at the entrance panel.

PRudenCe's eyes took on a mischievous gleam. "We have a vis'tor. Shall we let him in?"

Already smiling a welcome, AMitY turned to face the panel, expecting to see UNison. But the man looking in at her through the resinglas insert was much taller than PRudenCe's stocky friend, and instead of the light tan robe of an industrial laborer, he wore the forest green of an O'Zone Ranger.

V

MitY met ConCord's steady gaze through the door's resinglas insert and a suspicion crystalized in her mind. She turned to stare at her friend's flushed face. "It was *ConCord* who paid for the booth, wasn't it? You said it was a friend, and I thought—"

"I spoke Truth, AMitY. No matter what you 'lieve, Cit'zen Con-Cord *is* your friend. He c'tacted me last week and asked me to 'range this meet'n. I think you should listen to what he has to say."

"You can say that when you know what his father did to my parents?" AMitY demanded.

"He isn't 'sponsible for what his father does—"

"He's a Grissom, isn't he? And how did he know 'bout you, anyway? Has he been spy'n on me, gett'n 'ports from my ménage concierge and ed-visors? I thought you were my friend, PRudenCe. How could you let him talk you into this?"

PRudenCe's eyes clouded at the anger in AMitY's voice, but her voice was steady as she said, " 'Cause he really does have your best in'rests at heart, AMitY. You owe him the court'sy of—"

"I owe him noth'n—*noth'n!*"

"Keep your voice down," PRudenCe warned, glancing toward the street. "The Court'sy Guard checks these booths every half hour or so, look'n for illegal pairers. Maybe you'd better let Cit'zen ConCord in 'fore those swaphoppers in the next booth take Offense and 'port us."

AMitY shook her head stubbornly, and PRudenCe added, "Are you 'fraid you might weaken if you talk to him?"

AMitY suddenly found it difficult to meet her friend's clear eyes. Was PRudenCe right? *Was* she refusing to talk to ConCord because she didn't trust herself?

"Ver' well," she said coldly. "But he's *your* guest, 'member."

As PRudenCe let ConCord into the booth, AMitY assumed the Stance for Waiting. From the shadow of her cowl, she watched as ConCord bowed courteously, then presented her friend with a small packet of sweet wafers.

Why did he always seem so much larger than other men, she wondered crossly. And trust him to know about PRudenCe's weakness for sweets and to take advantage of it. How could he look so—so unruffled when she had given him Insult so many times? And why had he put in that bonding bid for her? Was he so sure of himself that he'd actually believed she would accept—or was this all some kind of high-status game? A way of amusing himself at the expense of a swarm girl?

"Live in Harmony, cit'zens." She'd almost forgotten how deep ConCord's voice was; something inside her quivered shamefully as he smiled at her. "Did you have time for a talk 'fore I got here?"

Despite her resolution to remain silent, AMitY couldn't resist the opening he'd given her. "We were talk'n 'bout the new Eugenics Code," she said, her voice so sweet that PRudenCe gave her a surprised look. "Isn't it lucky, I was just say'n, that the Code doesn't impose birth right 'strictions on the idle, 'though it does pen'lize cit'zens who had a 'cestor with some minor phys'cal d'fect six gen'rations back. If it were the other way 'round, half the Two-Name fam'lies in Old Town would be 'stinct by now, wouldn't they?"

She expected ConCord to take Offense—or at least to show embarrassment at her rudeness. She didn't expect him to give her rhetorical question a serious answer.

"You're prob'ly right, Cit'zen AMitY. The Eugenics Code isn't always equit'ble, but the line has to be drawn somewhere. The Panacea doesn't help those with degen'rate and generic disorders, and there's barely 'nough med'cal facil'ties now to handle accident victims. We have to find new methods to c'trol the birthrate. Our hydro-plants and O'Zone and Seafarms can't p'duce all the food we need—and where will we house new cit'zens in the future? Even if we had the build'n material for more swarms, where would we put them?"

"There's always the Parklands and the O'Zones." AMitY paused, then added slyly, "And 'course Old Town takes up a lot of space, doesn't it?"

"We're 'croach'n more and more upon the Parklands now," he said, ignoring the second part of her comment. "Someday there'll be no buffer at all 'tween us and the Outland Barriers. We haven't come to it yet, but we may have to curtail *all* new births for a period—and stop issu'n the Panacea to anyone not 'sential for maintain'n Order."

"Like the State does to cit'zens over fifty-five, no matter how p'ductive they are?" she said. "My grandfather was work'n on an improved strain of soybeans when he was sent to the Termine Wards. Surely, he should've been 'lowed to finish his research."

"I'm sorry—but it would disrupt Harmony and 'rouse Envy to make 'ceptions." ConCord's voice was so reasonable that AMitY wanted to throw the remains of her tea-treat in his face. "If the old didn't v'cate their 'signments, the young would stay Idle and that would be counter-Harmon'ous. Even the Council of Nine must step 'side when they reach Term'ation age. My grandfather 'linquished his chair on the Council to my father when he turned fifty-five."

"And where is your grandfather now?" she asked. "Did he go into a Termine ward like *my* grandfather did?"

This time she'd managed to penetrate ConCord's Control. A flush spread over his high-planed cheekbones. "You know my grandfather is still liv'n at Grissom House," he said quietly. "Does it make sense for him to take up space in the Termine wards when he can stay with us? Other fam'lies are 'lowed to keep their Termines with them, you know."

"*Old Town* fam'lies. *High-status* fam'lies. Not midstat or artisan fam'lies," AMitY pointed out.

ConCord flinched, and she knew her logic had stung. "You speak Truth, AMitY. I can't deny that the Code isn't always fair. But that doesn't alter the facts. Even if the Pancacea is withheld from ev'one and a mor'tor'um d'clared on any new births, that won't solve our 'med'ate problems. We should have started earlier to solve the pop'lation problem—"

He went on talking, and although AMitY didn't interrupt this time, she was tempted to tell him that she didn't need his lectures. After all, every school child knew that the discovery of the Universal Panacea had been a two-edged sword. A number of factors, including a series of so-called Cold Wars, had made massive population increases seem desirable to the world's industrialized nations. Followed by a decades-long period of mild weather and high food production, it had combined to create the anarchy of the period known as Chaos.

But that was old history, and AMitY didn't want to hear about past mistakes, especially not from a member of a privileged Old Town family. . . .

"—be honored if you'd 'cept, Cit'zen AMitY. I'll 'scort you, 'course."

The unusual formality in ConCord's voice brought AMitY back from her brooding. "What did you say? 'Rangements for *what,* Cit'zen ConCord?"

"I just 'vited you to 'tend the State Symphony with me 'morrow at Old Town Torium." ConCord flushed under her incredulous stare, but he went on doggedly. "The p'formance starts at 0400 Third Time. Since you're on Second Time, I offered to make 'rangements for an out-of-ménage pass for you with your concierge. And 'course I'll p'vide mo-cart trans'tation to and from Old Town."

AMitY opened her mouth for a sharp refusal. Unexpectedly, she was confronted with temptation. Even when her parents were alive, there'd never been enough tokes for tickets to the State Symphony. In fact, she'd never seen a live music performance of any kind—and she might never get another chance. To sit in the luxury of Old Town Torium, a fabled place she'd only heard about, to listen to a live performance of the best musicians in the State would be something to remember all her life ... did it *really* matter if she accepted just this one invitation from ConCord?

With a sharp thrill of anger, she realized the trap she'd almost fallen into. Although furious with herself, she was even more incensed with ConCord for being the instrument of her temptation. She pushed back her cowl so she could glare directly into his eyes. Although he must have been startled by her boldness, he didn't look away, and this only added fuel to her anger.

"The only in'tation I'd 'cept from you, Cit'zen ConCord-Grissom," she hissed, "is to 'tend a suicide party for your father, Cit'zen conSistency-Grissom."

Even before she heard PRudenCe's gasp and saw the color drain from ConCord's face, AMitY regretted her words. Although suicide was one private act the State hadn't been able to prevent (and some whispered that they didn't really want to), it was considered a Harmony Lapse to say the word aloud—or even to use the politer term: *self-termination.* It was known that parties sometimes preceded a citizen's suicide among those with high enough status to rate private quarters for entertaining. But to suggest that a citizen might throw one was a Gross Insult, punishable by loss of status and, in cases where malice could be proved, banishment to the Idle Swarms.

So AMitY waited for ConCord's reaction with a feeling of foreboding. She had just put a powerful weapon into his hands. Would he use it to pay her back for her many Insults? At the moment, his eyes registered nothing, which in itself was ominous. . . .

"You're a foolish girl, AMitY." ConCord's voice was whisper-soft, but it had a penetrating quality that made her flinch. "You're stubborn and unforgiv'n and c'sumed with bitterness. 'Stead of try'n to place the blame for your parents' deaths on my father, why don't you search your own heart for Truth? Your parents weren't martyrs who defied the Code out of a desire to help other cit'zens. They were Code Zealots, reactionaries who couldn't tol'rate change of any kind, not ev' when it was nec'sary to p'serve Order.

"The irony is that they ended up defy'n the Code themselves. The Code isn't perfect. It can't r'sist the strains pull'n it apart forev', but for now, it's the only adhesive hold'n us together. If your parents had gone to the Cit'zens' Ombudsman, used the proper channel for cit'zen dissent, 'stead of crit'z'n the new Eugenics Code in Public Forum, their 'pinions might have been listened to. Even so, they were given ev'ry op'tunity to 'pologize, and then use the proper channels. When they 'fused, my father, as Chief Arb'trator, had to pass judgment on them. I admit he could've chosen someth'n less severe. Perhaps he was wrong—but he felt he had to set an example."

He paused; when she maintained a stubborn silence, he went on, but now his voice had lost some of its cutting edge.

"I've never told you this before, AMitY, but I saw you earlier that day in the O'Zones. You were chas'n a butterfly, and your face was—was lit up, as if you'd been c'fined in Detention for a long time and were finally free. And later, when we talked, you looked me straight in the eyes, even though you must've been 'fraid. I knew then you were special, 'cause you still could dream, still ask questions, still search for answers.

I also knew that of all the girls I'd ever met, you were the only one who thought like me, who could help me 'chieve my dream of tear'n down the Barriers and let'n fresh air into this stagnant world of ours."

He paused again, this time to give her a searching look. "What happened to that girl, the one who wanted ev'body to have the op'tun'ty to splash in a stream of run'n water, to run free under the open sky, and to be 'lone when they felt the need for sol'tude? I don't know the girl you've become—bitter and full of 'sentment. You've done some reckless th'n's this past year, but to utter a Gross Insult to a cit'zen in the presence of a witness is pure folly. If you don't curb that foolish tongue of yours, you'll end up a drone in the Idles Swarms— and you'll only have yourself to blame."

He gave PRudenCe a stiff, unsmiling nod, murmured "Peace and Harmony, cit'zens," but he didn't look in AMitY's direction again before he turned and left the booth.

VI

o you think he'll 'port you?" There were anxiety lines between PRudenCe's finely arched eyebrows.

"He won't 'port me," AMitY said with as much confidence as she could muster. Since she couldn't control the slight tremor in her hands, she slid them up the loose sleeves of her robe. "And I'm not sorry I gave him Insult. Maybe now he'll b'lieve I don't want anyth'n more to do with him."

PRudenCe worried her lower lip with her teeth. "I know how you feel—or at least, I'm try'n to. But Cit'zen ConCord—well, he was really Out of Harmony when he left here. Maybe if you sent him a message and 'pologized—"

"I'll never 'pologize to that—that Two-Namer!"

PRudenCe winced. "Shhh . . . and 'just your cowl. You don't want to 'tract 'tention." She waited until AMitY, her lips tight, straightened her hood before she added, "If only you had 'cepted Cit'zen ConCord's bond'n bid, AMitY. With his Two-Name status, the Eugenics Board would surely allot you birth rights, even if—" She broke off, blinking hard.

"Even if my 'genics rat'n is 'provisional'? Well, it

was quad-A 'fore Cit'zen conSistency-Grissom sent my parents to the Sea Swarms. And there was a time when I would've 'cepted ConCord's bid gladly. But what you don't seem to un'stand is that ev' if I could forget he's a Grissom, how could I pos'bly share a Place of Being with his father, the man who was 'spons'ble for my parents' term'nation?"

And becasue she'd finally put into words the real reason for her stubbornness, AMitY's voice was tormented as she added, "Don't you see that I *can't* bond with ConCord, not when it means I'd have to live at Grissom House with my parents' murderer?"

PRudenCe's sigh held defeat. "Well, our half-hour's 'bout up, and it's still a ten-minute trek to the Comp Room from here. This is one day you don't dare be late, Cit'zen Amble-Along."

Despite her joke, PRudenCe's voice was so dispirited that AMitY felt ashamed. Next to the hopelessness of PRudenCe's future, her own problems seemed minor. The highest assignment PRudenCe could hope for was a service job in a swarm canteen or one of the Industrial Swarm factories. And even this would end when PRudenCe turned sixteen and was sterilized by the State. Very rarely were Steries afforded the privilege of work, and then only at some hotly-competed-for assignment in their own compound.

AMitY met her friend's clear eyes. Suddenly, she felt the need to comfort PRudenCe, to offer her some small gesture of friendship. Briefly, she struggled with her inhibitions, with the ban against touching; and then she reached out and, under cover of the waist-high partition, gave PRudenCe's hand a very quick, furtive squeeze.

PRudenCe's dark eyes filled with tears. AMitY

turned away quickly, embarrassed that her impulsive gesture had caused her friend to lose Control. .

With AMitY in the lead, the two girls left the privacy booth. A young couple was already waiting outside. Both wore the charcoal gray of porters; the containers cradled in the man's hands steamed faintly in the crisp winter air.

As AMitY plunged into the traffic, followed closely by PRudenCe, she speculated idly about the young couple. Most likely, it was a lovers' assignation by citizens not permitted, for one reason or another, an hour together in the privacy of a Government pairing unit. Would they take a chance and touch each other, perhaps even exchange a kiss behind the smoky resinglas? And if they were caught, would a few moments of intimacy be worth the punishment they could expect?

Unexpectedly, an image of ConCord came into her mind. There was a fluttering inside AMitY's chest, and a strange warmth invaded her body. If she had accepted his bonding bid, they would have the right to be alone, to touch each other—

She gave her head an angry shake, dispelling the unDisciplined image. She had made her decision, and it was the right one, the *only* one possible. Even if she could forget her vow, she could never live in the same house with Citizen consisTency-Grissom, the man who had passed such an unfair sentence upon her parents. Nothing could change that now. After today, it was unlikely her path would ever cross ConCord's again.

And why should the thought of never seeing ConCord again hurt so? It was something she wanted, didn't she? Not to be reminded of those months when she'd been so sure that they would bond someday and live out their lives together at Grissom House?

She glanced back at PRudenCe, who was matching her maneuvers through the lines of traffic, and was struck by the solemnity on her friend's usually cheerful face. Was PRudenCe still worried about what ConCord might do—or was it her own problems that troubled her? She had seen the young couple, too. Surely, it must have occurred to her that this was how she and UNison must meet in the future—a few illicit minutes together in a privacy booth when it could be arranged or when UNison, on his limited toke allotment, could afford it.

And how long would even that contract between them last? Although AMitY was sure UNison's devotion to her friend was genuine, she had her secret doubts that it was as strong as PRudenCe's. From the little she'd seen of UNison, she suspected he suffered from the Atavism of Personal Ambition. How long before he looked around for a girl with an acceptable eugenics rating to bond with, someone with enough status to rescue him from the bachelor ménages?

A space opened up beside her, and PRudenCe slid into it. AMitY met her friend's candid gaze, and because she already felt the pain of separation, this time she found it impossible to return PRudenCe's smile.

A few minutes later, they turned into one of the ingress corridors of the Education Complex. It was crowded with students, some going to classes, others headed for the Computer Room, with a sprinkling of yellow-robed ed-visors. Despite the ban on talking in the corridors, an undercurrent of whispers told AMitY that she wasn't alone in her private hopes—and fears.

When they reached the Computer Room, they fell in behind others of their classmates already queued up in front of the Life Assignment Computer. Although most maintained the Stance for Waiting, here and there someone moved restlessly or even forgot Decorum enough to chew on a thumbnail.

The student in front of AMitY, a stocky boy her own age, cleared his throat as if his mouth were dry. When his elbow brushed AMitY's robe, he gave her a quick bow of Apology.

Although AMitY returned the bow, the gesture was automatic. All her attention was focussed on the computer, a squat, rectangular console on the opposite side of the room. Behind its black panels, there was a whirring, pulsating sound, as if it were a living entity. She stared at a small crack near its message screen, aware that the muscles of her legs ached from the strain of trying not to break Stance.

She set herself the Discipline of repeating the Fourth Litany twice, and as the familiar words moved through her mind—*I will subjugate my will to the common good and to the judgment of my elders. / I will not complain nor gossip nor compete unduly. / Nor will I spread dissent*—her breathing returned to normal, and her tense body relaxed.

Every minute or so, as the students ahead of her received their assignment slips, AMitY shuffled forward a few inches. She watched covertly as, one by one, her classmates moved to the room's standing wall to read their slips, trying to guess which assignments had been Harmonious and which otherwise.

But even the faces of those whose cowls weren't lowered revealed nothing, and AMitY sighed inwardly, wishing her own Discipline training had been as effective. She willed the line to move faster; and then, paradoxically, when it did, was sorry she wouldn't have time to cant the Litany of Subjugation one more time before it was finally her turn to step forward, to tap out the letters and numbers of her Citizen's Identification Code on the computer keyboard.

Too numb now to feel anything, even hope, she waited as, deep inside the console, a humming started up and a thin slip of paper appeared in the output slot. She removed it with fingers that trembled disconcertedly, took one step backward for the customary bow of respect, then froze as a bell rang and red letters moved across the computer's message screen.

ABORT . . . ABORT . . . ABORT. . . .

Behind AMitY, there was a murmur of voices. As she stared at the red ribbon of letters, the piece of paper she was holding slipped from her nerveless fingers and fluttered to the floor. She was aware when PRudenCe scooped it up and handed it back to her, but even as she thrust it into her belt pouch, her eyes remained fixed on the computer.

With a whisper of sound, another slip of paper appeared in the output slot. She plucked it out, made the requisite bow, then moved quickly to an empty space in the standing wall before she looked down at the piece of paper in her hand. The printout letters on the card seemed blurred, and she had to blink hard before the words finally made sense:

CITIZEN IDENTIFICATION CODE: AM-5897-7688-Y (CN: *AMitY*)
LIFE ASSIGNMENT: Domestic Worker
REPORT TO: Grissom Museum House, Old Town, Quadrant 1, N'York State, N'Eastern States Of America, at 0200 Second Time, 22 Eleventh Month, Year 191 After Chaos
ATTENTION: Apply immediately for amended CIC tag pass at Peace Marshall's

Office. Courtesy Guard Headquarters, Civic
Swarm. Permission for three (3) Free-days is
granted.

AMitY felt the bitter taste of nausea at the back of
her throat. Rather than give in to it, she clenched her
teeth until they ached and fought the sickness to a
standstill. But she knew that no amount of Control
could erase the telltale anger from her face, so she bent
her head to let her cowl slip forward as bitter thoughts
assaulted her.

So *this* was how ConCord meant to punish her for
her Insult. After he'd left the privacy booth, he had
gone to the Education Complex to use his influence, as
only a Two-Namer could, to have her assigned to his
house as a domestic, knowing how humiliating it would
be to her. . . .

I won't do it, she thought hotly. *I'll petition the Citizen's Ombudsman to intervene and get my assignment changed. How can they make me serve in the house of my parents' murderer?*

But even as she raged inwardly, she knew that rebellion was useless, that there were no channels, not
even through the Citizens' Ombudsman, to repeal the
decision of the Life Assignment Computer, once it was
official.

VII

n the quad's Artisan Swarms, there was a relaxed atmosphere that both attracted and repelled more staid citizens. No matter what the hour, its arteries were always crowded with sightseers, with vendors, puppeteers, mime companies, and the fringe groups that were tolerated no other place in the quadrant.

AMitY turned into a main artery that would take her to HUmble's school, which was located in the heart of the swarm. Almost immediately, she was aware of a deepening of the street sound, of raised voices and open laughs, a laxness of the Courtesies. Even the appearance of the teeming crowd was different here, marked with signs of individuality usually kept hidden beneath a citizen's robe: a papier-mache flower boldly fastened to a cowl, a too-ornate belt, a bit of courting ribbon openly displayed on a young woman's wrist.

And in a line of privacy booths she was passing— she averted her eyes hastily, embarrassed and yet fascinated by the sight of three citizens, their cowls pushed back, laughing and gesturing behind the smoky resinglas while in another, a couple stood so close together that she knew they must be touching behind the waist-high partition.

As she passed a cluster of vendor's stalls, which displayed the crafts permitted to the swarm's artisans, she caught glimpses of hand-decorated sandals, belts and pouches woven from sea-kelp, personal adornments meant for private ménage wear. There were also poems and stories and even opinion tracts (some of which, it was said, bordered on Dissent), handwritten on scrolls of reprocessed paper.

Her step slowed as she tried to get a better look at an ink drawing wall scroll. The citizen shuffling behind her bumped her from the rear, but instead of the hiss of Offense she deserved, the man, who wore the maroon robes of an artisan, smiled dreamily and murmured a soft "Harmony, sweet Cit'zen," before he slid into an opening in another lane.

A few cross-streets farther, AMitY began the intricate turning maneuver that eventually brought her to the entrance of HUmble's school. As she moved along the ingress corridor toward the common rooms, she noted that even here small signs of the relaxed attitude of the Artisan Swarms were evident. The cowls of some of the students were pushed back, revealing their fresh, animated faces, and it was obvious that few of them bothered to observe the stricter rituals of Courtesy—except when a yellow-robed ed-visor was in sight.

As AMitY waited for her brother in the school's noisy visiting room, she couldn't help wondering what would have happened to HUmble if he'd been sent to the stricter Common Swarm schools. With his unbridled curiosity, he was always under restriction, even here in the tolerant Artisan Swarms.

And what did the future hold for him? So far, his

grades and high intelligence had protected him some-
what—but what if his ed-visors finally gave up on him
and declared him an Incorrigible? If he were transferred to the Idle Swarms, what would happen to his
natural exuberance? How long before he joined one of
the secret dissident groups, became a Rad and ended
up in the Sea Swarms?

"Harmony, Cit'zen Big Sister," HUmble said at
her elbow. Although he spoke in the proper whisper, his
eyes were bright with excitement. Like the grandfather
they both resembled so much, his hair was a vibrant red
and his eyes were a deep aquamarine. A little small for
his age, he had the thin, intense face of a scholar, and
AMitY felt an Atavistic urge to reach out and push
back the unruly curls that tumbled over his wide forehead.

"Harmony to you, too, Cit'zen Little Brother," she
said, smiling at him. "Thank you for the Comp Day
message. I have to admit it was a s'prise. I didn't realize
you were so prosp'rous."

HUmble's eyes slid away. "Oh, I don't tell you
ev'thing," he mumbled. Before AMitY could pursue
the question of his surprising prosperity further, he
added hastily, "I hope your 'signment was Harmon'ous,
AMitY. Did you get into the Tenners?"

In her pleasure of seeing him, she had almost forgotten her disappointment and anger. Now, as it all
came rushing back, she had to force herself to smile into
his eager face, to speak calmly.

"Not the Tenners—but someth'n ver' Har-
mon'ous. I've been 'signed as a 'mestic at Grissom Museum House. Just think of the marvels I'll get to see in
Old Town—"

As she went on talking, embellishing the advantages of her assignment, there was an odd look on HUmble's face that made him suddenly appear very mature.

"Did Cit'zen ConCord have an'th'n to do with this?" he interrupted.

"I'm not sure," AMitY answered honestly. "It—it's a great op'tun'ty for a Common Swarms student."

"But what 'bout the Tenners? You had such good grades."

"Not in the Disciplines," she reminded him. "And that should be a lesson to *you*, Cit'zen HUmble. A few more Rep'mands and you won't even be 'lowed to take your Elevenses."

"I hate the Disciplines," HUmble burst out rebelliously. "There's so much to learn 'bout history and science and math, and yet we waste half our time on those moldy ol' Litanies!"

"Shhh ... do you want to go on 'port again?" AMitY glanced around the visiting room uneasily. " 'Sides, it's much worse in the Commons schools—and what if they sent you to the Idles? The Disciplines are *all* they teach there."

"I know—but wouldn't it be dilly if you could study what you like?" His small face was wistful. "Sometimes I dream 'bout a place where there's lots of space so you can be 'lone when you want. The A'aludes call it E'ewere. I think that's their word for Elsewhere, but I'm not sure. It could mean Sanctuary, too. Lots of their words mean two things."

"The A'aludes?" AMitY had finally found her voice.

"The little people—or at least, I think they're people. That's their name for themselves. It means—well, people."

"How do you know that?" she said; she was finding it hard to breathe.

"Oh, I watch them sometimes. And I listen to the sing'n and storytell'n, too." His eyes were dreamy. "At first, I didn't un'stand what they said, but then I 'covered that their words are like ours only they say them dif'rent. I wish I could talk to them but 'course, you can't do that in a dream."

"How long has this been go'n on?"

"Oh, it started just 'fore I came to the Artisan Swarms." He gave her a defiant look. "I know we aren't 'spose to talk 'bout dreams, but Cit'zen ConCord said ev'body has dreams and—" He broke off abruptly, ducking his head so his cowl slipped forward to hide his face.

"ConCord's been here to see you? But why—" She stopped then as a realization came to her. Of course— where else would HUmble, with his allotment account always in arrears, get the tokes to pay for a Comp Day message?

"I'm sorry, AMitY." HUmble looked so miserable that she didn't have the heart to be angry with him. "I know how you feel 'bout Cit'zen ConCord—but he's really ding-dong, you know. My class thinks it's top-o, hav'n a Parkie come here to see me."

"He's been here more than once?"

"Oh, lots of times." Now that HUmble knew that she wasn't going to scold him, he had regained his usual aplomb. "He always brings me someth'n—sweet ice or soy-tein wafers or dried fruit. He gives the school books, too—and one time a mag'fy'n glass for my science class."

AMitY understood a few things that had puzzled her, such as why HUmble's escapades had been tolerated by his ed-visors. "What do you talk 'bout?" she asked, curious in spite of herself.

"Oh—th'n's. He talks 'bout you sometimes. And we talk 'bout an'mals and history and what it's like in the O'Zones." He gave her a tentative smile. "He said he—he wanted you to have a whiz Comp Day, which is why I let him pay for the message. Are you Out of Harmony with me, AMitY?"

"Not with you. But ConCord-Grissom isn't really our friend. We don't need his gifts."

When HUmble looked as if he wanted to argue with her, she changed the subject and asked him a question about school. HUmble was soon giving her a detailed account of the chemistry experiment that had proved so disastrous.

Although AMitY listened with outward attentiveness, her mind was on HUmble's dreams. How was it possible for two people to share the same dream? Was it some kind of inherited insanity that manifested itself at puberty? AMitY discovered her mouth was dry. What if the authorities found out she and HUmble were having identical dreams? If they decided it was a mental aberration, she and HUmble would be sterilized and sent to the Sterie Swarms. . . .

Suddenly, she knew there was too much danger inherent in what she'd just learned to keep it to herself. And the only person she could safely go to was her grandfather. Luckily, she would be visiting him tomorrow. Of course, private conversations were impossible in the crowded Termine wards, but surely she could think of a way to get his opinion without putting herself and HUmble in danger.

And if her grandfather couldn't help her, then she would have to live with it, to teach HUmble how reckless it was to talk about such things. One thing she would never do was submit to sterilization—and life in the Sterie Swarms. And she would never allow HUmble to suffer that fate either, not even if it meant doing something desperate—like escaping with him into the Outlands.

As always when she visited her grandfather, AMitY felt a crushing depression as she wended her way through the close-packed cots of his ward. Even the comparative privacy of a meditation room was denied the Termines, since every inch of space was needed for the overflow of cots. That there were other deprivations, she also knew. Although her grandfather never complained, she was aware that it was specially hard for him to live without mental stimulation. Which made it all the more re-markable that he always remained the same, as if he drew upon some inner fountain of strength to keep himself from succumbing to the apathy of the wards.

AMitY caught sight of him now and smiled to herself. He was sitting cross-legged on his cot, absorbed in the book he was holding in his lap. He had pushed back his privacy cowl, and his hair, only slightly less vivid than her own, stood out like a beacon in the drabness of the low-ceilinged room.

As she often did, AMitY wondered at the incon-gruity of her grandfather's name. *ausTere* . . . he was anything but that, with his quick smile, his eyes that looked so young, belying his fifty-seven years. Surely, there must be something wrong with a Code that al-lowed such a fine, keen mind to stagnate in a Termine ward.

Her grandfather looked up, his eyes still unfocussed. Then, as he recognized AMitY, his narrow face broke into a warm smile. He slid off the cot and rose—but not, she noted, until he had carefully closed the book he'd been reading and placed it at the foot of the cot.

"Peace and Harmony, Granddaughter AMitY," he said. "I've been 'spect'n you."

"Harmony, Grandfather ausTere." She gave him a deep bow before she gestured toward the book. "Such lux'ry—have you been gambl'n in the Artisan Swarms?"

Citizen ausTere smiled absently at her little joke. "It's a reproduction of a pre-Chaos history book. A friend lent it to me." Avoiding her eyes, he smoothed out the sleep cocoon that covered the webbing of his cot, making a place for her to sit down.

AMitY didn't bother to ask him the name of his friend. Who but ConCord did her grandfather know who possessed such a valuable object as a complete book?

"Was your 'signment Harmon'ous, AMitY?" AMitY read her grandfather's concern in his eyes.

"Much better than I deserve," she said, giving the standard answer. "I've been 'signed to Grissom Museum House as a 'mestic."

Citizen ausTere was silent for a moment. "I see—yes, I see," he said finally. "Grissom House has a fine library. Perhaps you'll be 'lowed book priv'leges."

"That would be ver' Harmon'ous."

Citizen ausTere gave her a sharp look. "Th'n's work out for the best, AMitY. As your father so rightly 'minded me on my Termine Day, 'Each of us has his own place in the great design of the Order.'"

Although his words were pious, AMitY caught the dryness in his voice and found herself smiling, remembering that her father had always been able to find a quote from the Litanies for every occasion. Had Con-Cord been right about her parents? Had they been Zealots, too reactionary to accept even the smallest change in the Code? One thing she knew for sure: she never could have told either of them about the dreams—or about the visions. But she *could* get her grandfather's opinion—provided they had a little privacy.

Surreptitiously, she glanced around the ward. Although no one was watching them openly, she knew that every word they exchanged was being monitored by every citizen within earshot of their low-pitched voices.

Not that she blamed them for eavesdropping. In this drab, sterile place, without even holovision privileges to distract them, every visitor who came to the ward was a welcome diversion. But it also meant that she would have to be very careful what she said to her grandfather.

"Grandfather, I have a puzzle for you to solve," she said, instantly earning his attention. "A ménage-mate of mine has a fragment of a pre-Chaos book. I know you used to read a lot when the State Library was still open to private cit'zens, so I thought you might be able to tell us the end'n."

"Do you know the book's title?" Citizen ausTere's eyes were alight with interest.

"The cover and the title page are miss'n, but it's obv'ously a work of fiction. The—the hero has strange dreams 'bout 'nother place he calls E'ewere."

"What do you mean by ' 'nother place'?"

"A different world. The sun is 'scribed as be'n more golden than our sun, and there are four blue moons—so bright that they can be seen clearly in the daytime. Have you ever read of such a planet?"

"E'ewere, you say? It's not in our solar system. I 'spect your friend's book is someth'n called science fiction. In my youth, I was quite 'dicted to it. This was 'fore our wise Council outlawed spec'lative fiction as Decadent." Again, Citizen ausTere's voice held wryness. "You say the hero went to this place? By some manner of space-travel'n vehicle?"

"No, the fragment spoke of dreams so vivid they 'peared to be real. Then he started see'n E'ewere while he was 'wake. A glow would form 'round a nearby door, and then, through the light, he could see this place. It seemed so real that he was sure that if he stepped through, he would be in E'ewere."

"A time portal—or a matter transmitter," Citizen ausTere said, nodding. "Yes, the old writers spoke of such things in their works of fiction."

"You mean such a thing is pos'ble?"

"Not to our technol'gy or even to pre-Chaos science, but the'ret'cally—yes, there's a pos'bil'ty that matter can be transmitted through space and re'sembled at t'other end." He regarded her thoughtfully. "This place—was it 'habited?"

"The pages 'scribed winged creatures. Very small and prim'tive, but 'tell'gent 'nough to have a language."

"Wings, you say? They would have to be as hollow-boned as birds to be able to fly—at least if the gravity there was the same as Earth's. Unless they had no nat'ral en'mies, such creatures couldn't survive—and without such en'mies, they would prolif'rate till they 'shausted their food. No, not very plasu'ble, your story, but still—yes, intrigu'n."

"And the dreams, the visions? How do you s'pose the writer 'splained that? There was someth'n more. 'Nother character, the sister of the hero, had the same dreams."

Citizen ausTere tapped his upper lip with his forefinger. "I once read of a pre-Chaos machine that 'corded the 'lectrical waves of the human brain. Perhaps the portal to E'ewere was 'tuned to their brain wave pattern. Be'n siblings, they would share the same hered'ty." He thought a moment, then shook his head. "But such simple people couldn't have 'veloped such marvels of science—did the writer give these beings a name?"

"He called 'em A'aludes."

"Well, a device like a time portal would only be pos'ble for a ver' 'vanced race. I wonder how the writer solved it—too bad more of the book didn't s'vive." He smiled at AMitY. "This is a ver' int'rest'n problem. Perhaps I can come up with a theory for your ménage-mate by your next visit."

He tapped his knuckles together, a habit that she knew denoted concern. "And you'll soon be 'port'n to Grissom House to begin your duties as a 'mestic." He gave her a long, sober look. "There's no Harmony in look'n back, Granddaughter. And no cit'zen is 'spons'ble for what his parents do."

When AMitY was silent, he sighed under his breath. To her relief, he changed the subject. "What's new with Cit'zen PRudenCe? I trust her 'signment was Harmon'ous?"

"She's been 'signed to an Apprendice Swarm for canteen workers. We're go'n to spend our last Free-day together in the common rooms of her ménage." She tried for a smile. "It may be the last time. PRudenCe'll be sixteen soon."

"I un'stand—yes, I do un'stand."

His face was so troubled that she hastened to say, "I haven't thanked you yet for the Comp Day message."

But now it was her grandfather's turn to look away. His reaction was so much like HUmble's that she realized ConCord must have subsidized another of her Comp Day messages. Only the knowledge that this would be her last visit with her grandfather for a long time kept her from showing resentment.

On the long trek back to the Common Swarms, AMitY asked herself several questions. Why had Con-Cord seen that she had several Comp Day messages? Was it really because he wanted her to have a "whiz" Comp Day? And why had he wasted so much time on a Termine and a non-stat student? Was it guilt because his father had deprived HUmble of his parents—and her grandfather of his daughter and son-in-law?

Somehow, this seemed unlikely. After all, Con-Cord had defended his father's decision. He had called her parents Code Zealots and had laid the responsibility of their deaths upon their own shoulders. More likely, her earlier suspicions were right and he was playing a game with her for his own amusement.

Well, in the future, there would be no more book loans for her grandfather, no more visits to HUmble's school, no more fruit wafers for PRudenCe's sweet tooth. And how would he treat *her* in the future? Surely, he would take every opportunity to humiliate her. Why else had he arranged for her to be apprendiced as a domestic at Grissom House?

AMitY lowered her cowl to shield her face from the eyes of passersby. In her anger, she made herself another vow. No matter what lay ahead, she would never apologize to ConCord, never give him the satisfaction of knowing that his tactics had succeeded, that finally, at this late date, she was sorry that she had given him—and his father—Insult.

VIII

fficially, the houses of Old Town, where the Council of Nine and other Two-Name families lived, were State museums, maintained from public funds; but only occasionally were their public viewing rooms open, and then by invitation only, to ordinary citizens. On the occasion when AMitY's family ménage had been invited there by ConCord, she'd been awed by the grandeur of the four-storied red brick building with its multi-gabled roof and extravagance of windows, so rare in a windowless society; by its wealth of precious wood-paneling and antique furnishings, its library of pre-Chaos books.

At the time, she had thought that to live in such a place must be a little like the old heaven myth. But today, as she showed her pass to a scarlet-robed Courtesy Guardsman at the domestics' entrance, she felt as if she were walking into a trap, especially when the heavy door slammed shut behind her.

An older woman, who wore the teal-blue robe of a domestic, introduced herself as Citizen DiligEnce. Bustling and talkative, she pointed out a flight of narrow stairs which, she told AMitY, the domestics must always use.

"It's the first rule of Grissom House that the 'mestic staff never 'trudes 'pon the priv'cy of the Fam'ly," she said sternly.

That there were other rules, AMitY soon found out. Citizen DiligEnce ran through a whole litany of them as they climbed three flights of stairs to the domestics' quarters.

"Cit'zen fruGality, the chief 'mestic, runs a ver' proper house. If you've been 'spect'n a sloddy 'signment, you'll be dis'pointed, young cit'zen. Unlike *some* Old Town Houses I could name, we 'serve the Court'sies here at all times. New 'prendices are 'signed duties in the 'mestic quarters for the first year. It'll be a long time 'fore you're trusted near the family quarters or the public view'n rooms."

She paused on the stairs to look back at AMitY, her eyes not unfriendly. "You'll find this a good 'signment, 'vided you do your work prop'ly. We're all on Second Time, and the mistress is ver' 'sid'rate. Nat'ral food for second- and thirdmeals, fruit twice a week, mattresses on our bunks, fresh robes ev'ry other day— and not your rough, Common Swarms robes, either." She gave AMitY's robe a caustic look. "Freedays ev' week; Parklands, Menag'rie or Museum priv'leges three times a year. So do your work and mind your Court'sies, and maybe you'll please Cit'zen fruGality in spite of—"

She didn't finish the sentence, maybe because they had reached the top of the stairs. AMitY barely had time to stow her few private possessions away in the locker she'd been assigned before she was summoned into the presence of the chief domestic.

She knew, as soon as she entered the office, that somehow she had already incurred the dislike of the woman who was sitting behind a small desk, making chalk marks next to a list of names on a large lap slate. Although Citizen fruGality must have heard the door open and close, she didn't look up.

Her robe, made of finer material than the one Citizen DiligEnce wore, was the same teal-blue, Otherwise, AMitY would have thought, from the woman's haughty demeanor, her atypically long fingernails, and the expensive metal frame that held her CIC tag, that she was a member of the Grissom family.

Even when Citizen frugaLity continued to ignore her, AMitY refused to fall into the pitfall of curiosity. Although she wanted to study the room's metal storage cabinet, the black-and-white scrolls extolling the virtue of hard work and frugality on the wall, the glass-fronted case that held several tattered books and a pile of slates, she kept her eyes fixed on the chief domestic.

After a while, as if her stillness was an irritant, Citizen frugaLity looked up. With no pretense at Courtesy, she examined AMitY from cowl to sandals. Like her hands, her face was long and narrow, and when she spoke finally, her upper lip quivered as if her own words had a bitter taste.

"It seems you're here at the *personal* r'quest of Cit'zen ConCord-Grissom," she said. "So we'll see if we can't find a proper place for such a *favored* 'prendice. Your first duties will be in the laundry and as a scrubbee in the 'mestic canteen and common rooms."

She paused to judge the effect of her words. Prudently, AMitY murmured, "I un'stand, Cit'zen frugaLity."

"And we don't p'mit any frivol'ties at Grissom

House. The mistress is ver' strict. If you want holovision and other priv'leges, you'll have to forget such Van'ties as pinch'n your cheeks like an Idle Swarm pleasure woman."

AMitY kept her face expressionless, sensing that to explain that her coloring was natural would be a waste of time. Why did the woman dislike her so? Was it because of ConCord's intervention?

Citizen deCOrum, the concierge at her ménage, had once told her that patronage was a way of life among Old Town domestic staffs. As one of the few assignments not under the control of the Life Assignment Computer, the position of domestic was often passed down to the relatives and ménage-mates of the staff. Had she inadvertently upset some plan of Citizen frugaLity's?

"Since you're such a *special* case, you'll be under my 'rect sup'vision. You can be sure I'll keep a ver' close eye 'pon you, Cit'zen AMitY. And I see no reason why you shouldn't start right to work in the energy room. I'm sure Cit'zen seRenity will welcome a strong young cit'zen at the energy wheels to help 'plenish the menage bat'ries."

She dismissed AMitY with a wave of her hand.

AMitY bowed stiffly. "Peace and Harmony, Cit'zen frugaLity." She turned and started for the door, eager to escape from Citizen frugaLity's hostility. But before she reached it, the woman's voice, silky-smooth now, stopped her.

"If you have any 'plaints, I s'gest you think twice 'fore you bother Cit'zen ConCord with them. I received my 'structions this morn'n. It seems you're sadly lack'n in the Disciplines. I'm to make sure you 'serve strict standards of Decorum at Grissom House."

AMitY read the satisfaction in the woman's thin-lipped smile and knew that Citizen frugaLity had deliberately waited until now to reveal her knowledge that AMitY was in disfavor with ConCord. Although she wished it were possible to tell the woman that under no circumstances would she ever complain to Citizen ConCord about *anything,* she bowed silently and went to report to the energy room.

During the next few days, she was careful to give no cause for complaint. With her superiors—and as the newest apprendice, everybody on the staff was that—she observed every nuance of Courtesy, did what she was told as quickly and competently as possible, and spoke only when spoken to first—and even then she weighed every word she said.

At baytime, when she was preparing for bed in the sleep alcove she shared with three other apprendices, she was aware that her cove-mates were watching her with more than normal curiosity, confirming her suspicions that rumors about her association with ConCord were already rampant. But it was only when she overheard a bit of gossip between two of the younger domestics that she learned the real cause for Citizen frugaLity's hostility.

She was in the basement laundry room, folding clean robes, when two of the domestics clattered down the service stairs. The low drone of the sonic-cleaner covered the rustling sounds AMitY was making at the folding table in one dimly lighted corner. The women, intent upon their gossip, didn't notice her as they came into the room, their arms piled high with soiled sleep cocoons.

"—can't b'lieve Cit'zen ConCord is really in'rested in pair'n with *that* one, no matter what Cit'zen seReniTy says." The speaker was AMitY's age, the one with a round, pasty face that always reminded AMitY of an uncooked soytein wafer.

"She's a strange one, y'know. The first day Cit'zen AMitY was here, Cit'zen dEportUre sent her to the laundry room, like she always does new 'prendices. Ev'body was wait'n for her to come fly'n back up the stairs when she found out she was 'lone down here, but no, she was cool as Thirteenth month. Stayed down till she'd finished the chore Cit'zen dEportUre'd give her and then came upstairs to ask what she should do next."

The other girl shuddered. "It's unnatural, that's what it is. I 'member when it happened to me. I couldn't stop shak'n till Cit'zen dEportUre gave me a cup of hot water and let me lie down on my bunk." She gave a shaky laugh. "Let's hurry. I don't like it down here, ev' with a trek mate."

But the other girl's mind was still on the new apprendice. "Whatev' the truth 'bout her and Cit'zen ConCord, Cit'zen frugaLity is really Out of Harmony with her. She had ev'th'n 'ranged so the niece of one of her old ménage-mates would get the 'signment when Cit'zen TRUstworthy reached Termine age."

"Well, if you ask me—"

But whatever the girl had been about to add was left unsaid. She looked around just then, saw AMitY standing behind the folding table, and her mouth formed a round *O* of dismay. Silently, AMitY picked up a pile of robes and went out, deriving satisfaction from the consternation she was leaving behind. For a change, she thought angrily as she started up the service stairs, let someone else worry about being reported for *their* Lapses.

But her anger subsided quickly as she thought over the conversation she'd overheard. Obviously, it was some kind of joke, sending the new domestics down to the laundry room alone—and, of course, her reaction had disappointed them. Did they think she was especially brave—or did they suspect she was a Deviate, a throwback who didn't mind being alone? Maybe if she had gone into hysterics, she might have won some kind of acceptance from the other domestics.

She felt a soul-wrenching loneliness suddenly. No matter how hard she worked, how rigidly she observed the Courtesies, she would make no friends here, not as long as Citizen frugaLity was chief domestic of Grissom House.

Lost in her thoughts, she reached the next landing, opened the door with her free hand and went through. She was halfway down the hall before she realized that she'd made a mistake and was on the wrong floor. Although the hall was dark, light from a window at the far end revealed a collection of ancient, museum quality travel posters expensively framed in gleaming metal on the walls, and she knew she was in the family section of the house.

She made a vexed sound and started to turn—just as a door opened nearby. Her mouth went dry as she recognized the tall man in hunter-green who stepped out into the hall. She had the presence of mind to give ConCord a stiff bow, letting her privacy cowl fall forward to hide her flushed face.

ConCord returned the bow—just barely. She would've believed he was indifferent to their meeting if she hadn't seen how his jaw muscles tightened before he stalked off.

AMitY stared after him, angry and frustrated because she'd rehearsed so carefully how she would snub ConCord the first time he spoke to her, only to have him snub her first. She started back down the hall; then, realizing that ConCord had left the door open behind him, she gave into temptation and stopped to look inside.

The room was large, sparsely furnished with antiques AMitY knew must be priceless—a metal desk, several real-wood chairs, a narrow table, and a chest of drawers that was the size of several citizens' lockers. Her breath left her in a long sigh as she saw the books, each encased in its own protector, that filled a shelf on one wall. One chair, its seat covered with worn, but rare woven fabric, was pulled up to the desk. A book lay open on the desk, and again yielding to curiosity, she slipped into the room and bent over it.

It was a geography book—or at least, the page was open to a map. Since the light was so poor, she couldn't make out the caption underneath, but the outline had a vaguely familiar look and she finally recognized it as a map of pre-Chaos N'York State, so many times larger than the present one.

AMitY's arms tightened around the stack of robes she was holding. At one time, she had been deeply involved with ConCord's plans for an expedition into the Outlands. Now, if the trek should materialize, the information would come to her second-hand, through household gossip or on the common room newscaster.

She straightened, her gaze lingering on the shelf of books, and unconsciously, she sighed again. To live with such treasures every day—and then to talk about citizens' equality! What a hypocrite the man was—and how lucky for her that she'd found ConCord out before she'd accepted his bonding bid.

She started for the door, only to find that she was no longer alone. Citizen frugaLity, her eyes snapping, was standing in the doorway.

"So you've decided to defy me, have you, cit'zen?" Although the woman's lips barely moved, her sibilant whisper seemed to fill the room. "Were you look'n for Cit'zen ConCord? Well, he doesn't want to hear your 'plaints. And I have my orders. At the first sign of 'bellion, your priv'leges are to be s'pended. There'll be no more holovision for you—or games or reading, either. In the future, you'll spend your free time, what little you have, in your sleep 'cove, cant'n the Litanies."

AMitY sensed the futility of explaining that she'd lost her way in the unfamiliar house, that she'd had no intention of seeking out ConCord. Citizen frugaLity had been looking for an excuse to Reprimand her—and now she had it. It would only exacerbate the trouble to make excuses.

So she remained silent when Citzen frugaLity added, "You'll work four hours extra ev'ry day at the energy wheels when your reg'lar duties are finished, and I'm sure we can find other ways to teach you the folly of status-climb'n, Cit'zen AMitY."

But it was with a rebellious heart that she bowed her head, thus accepting both the Reprimand and the punishment. During the next few days, as she went about the duties Citizen frugaLity piled upon her, she sometimes felt like a shadow, flitting around the edges of life at Grissom House. Even the meager Courtesies that she'd received as a new apprendice were denied her now. Except for Citizen frugaLity, no one spoke to her; no one acknowledged her presence, not even her three 'cove-mates.

When she went into the common room or canteen or laundry room to perform her numerous duties, heads bent closer together and voices lowered, and she wondered if Citizen frugaLity had given orders to the staff not even to allow her the diversion of eavesdropping.

AMitY's pride sustained her now. Determined not to give any legitimate reason for complaint, she did the chores assigned her, and when the chief domestic chided her for some imaginary infraction, she accepted the abuse in silence. Each day, after her work shift was through and the other domestics were free to watch holovision, to play games or read, she reported to the energy room where she put in four more hours, pumping away at the energy wheels until her legs jerked and throbbed with fatigue.

Officially, no citizen could be forced to produce more energy than they used, a wise rule that precluded slavery, just as no citizen except Termines and Undesirables could be deprived of the Universal Panacea. So it was only her pride that prevented AMitY from complaining to the Citizens' Ombudsman, as she rightfully could have. Her only satisfaction was the knowledge that her fortitude was earning her the grudging respect of the other domestics—and that it was a great disappointment to Citizen frugaLity.

As the days, then the weeks inched past, she grew increasingly restless, especially when no messages came from her relatives or PRudenCe. She was sitting alone in a corner of the canteen, eating her thirdmeal of fish broth and soytein wafers, when it occurred to her that the chief domestic had the power to withhold any personal messages that came for her. The suspicion depressed her, and for once, she paid no attention to the whispers and glances that followed her as she finished her meal, then dropped her bowl and dish into the sterilizer and left the canteen.

Her feet seemed unusually heavy as she returned to her sleep alcove. Somehow, the knowledge that she'd done nothing to deserve such treatment was a poor solace this evening. Ironically, even her old recurrent dream seemed to have deserted her since she'd come to Grissom House. When she did dream, she had nightmares that wrenched her awake, her heart pounding, her body covered with sweat. Sometimes, it was PRudenCe she dreamed about; sometimes it was her grandfather or HUmble, but always she was forced to stand by helplessly while they were caught up in some disaster, all the more terrifying because she couldn't remember what the danger was after she awakened.

When she reached the alcove, she climbed up to her bunk, too apathetic to brush out her hair and undress. With her feet dangling over the side, she sat staring down at the floor. If only she had something to read—but then, even if she were allowed access to the domestics' small library, it would be impossible to read in the dark alcove with its one authorized safety light.

Although traditionally called an alcove, it was really a small, separate room, with four walls instead of the usual partitions, open top and bottom for ventilation. A musty odor permeated the room, making AMitY suspect that the fourth floor had once have been a storage attic before its division into compartments to accommodate the domestic staff. Each alcove was large enough to hold two double-bunks; unlike those in the Family and Common Swarms, thin mattresses rested across the webbing, cushioning the sleep cocoons.

AMitY's robe whispered around her as she changed to a cross-legged position on the bunk and assumed the Stance for Meditation—head bowed, hands palm-up on her knees, eyes closed. To calm her overactive mind, she canted the most soothing of the Litanies, the first one taught to children when they were old enough to talk. But today, the words (*I am one, one of many . . .*) seemed more of an irritant than a solace.

For one thing, there was so much light against her closed eyelids that it was hard to concentrate on the words of the Litany. . . .

Light? Here in her sleep alcove?

AMitY's eyes flew open; her breath caught sharply when she saw the amber rays that streamed from the ceiling a few feet above her head. Although she'd spent many hours staring up at the particular patch of ceiling, she'd never seen it in full light before. Now she realized that what she'd taken for deep cracks in the aging plaster was in reality a small, square trapdoor. Decades earlier, it must have been painted the same grayish white as the ceiling, but when she reached up hesitantly and touched it, it felt smooth under her fingertips, unlike the rough plaster that surrounded it.

And the light—it crept through the cracks around the trapdoor, filling the room with a golden mist. For a long time, she sat there staring, entranced by the dust motes that swirled in the stream of light. Random wisps of thought and half-formed images filled her mind as the light ebbed and flowed, almost as it were signalling her, coaxing her to come closer. . . .

She knew that if she closed her eyes and said the Litanies from beginning to end, she could banish the light as she'd done so many times before. But did she really want to send it away? After all, why should she? The hunger for diversion was so strong, and the light was so friendly, so reassuring. . . .

Was it a hallucination? Or could it possibly be something else? Her grandfather had speculated that it was a window (a portal, he'd called it) through which she could view another world. Even if it were real, how could it be any more dangerous than watching the three-dimensional figures on a holovision stage? What harm would there be in simply *looking?*

AMitY rose to a crouching position. The webbing under her mattress groaned a protest as she stood up, balancing herself carefully so she wouldn't fall. When she pushed against the square of wood above her head, tiny flakes of old paint rained down upon her upturned face, and at first the square of wood refused to budge. Then, with a wrenching sound, the paint that held it fast yielded to pressure and it swung upward, releasing a flood of light into the alcove.

AMitY grasped the edges of the opening with her fingers. She hoisted her body through and found herself crouching in an oddly shaped space, too small to be called a room. From the peaked ceiling just a few feet above her head, she guessed that this must once have been one of the roof cupolas, blocked off as unusable space when the attic was converted into living quarters.

Not wanting to be caught here by one of her 'cove-mates, she turned and lowered the trapdoor before she examined her surroundings more closely, discovering then that the source of the light was a small arched window set under the eaves.

For a long time she studied the window, admiring the tiny bits of colored glass that formed a stylized pattern of roses. As she stared, the pattern seemed to shift, reforming into something else. Was it an illusion, the artistry of the long-dead craftsman who had created the stained glass window? Or was the glass actually moving, changing?

She inhaled deeply to steady herself before she made her way to the window, stepping carefully upon the old floor boards. As if keeping time with her own racing pulses, the light intensified, ebbed, then intensified again as she drew near. Even before she reached it, the window glass, with its pattern of roses, had dissolved away completely.

Somehow, when she was close enough to touch the sill, she wasn't surprised to find that she was staring into the place of her dreams, into the world that HUmble had called E'ewere.

or a long time, AMitY crouched at the window, her eyes fixed on the scene spread out before her.

High above a wide valley, in fact, completely surrounding it, were jagged mountains, a grim expanse of gray rock that seemed to hold a chill, even at a distance. But there was nothing grim or forbidding about the valley itself. Although its sloping sides were strewn with huge boulders, with great outcroppings of the same gray rock of the cliffs, its groves of trees and its lush, emerald-green covering of mosslike grass was incredibly beautiful to AMitY's color-starved eyes. It also looked very real, as if she could reach out and touch the glossy leaves of a nearby bush and feel the warmth of its golden sun against her skin.

She became aware of sound—tinkling, musical, far away. Was it a bell ringing—or was that singing she heard? If she listened hard enough, maybe she could make out words. . . .

With a start, she realized that she'd almost fallen into the very trap she'd warned herself against. She clenched her hands until her fingernails bit into her palms and told herself that she mustn't make the mistake of believing that what she saw was real. She would look, feast her eyes, even listen, since the illusion included sound. This far she would go—but no further.

To give in completely to this aberration of her own too-imaginative mind would be insanity. She knew, every citizen knew, what happened to the insane in a world where the slightest deviation from the normal was considered a threat to the Status Quo. So she mustn't forget, not for a second, that this was a mirage, a dream without substance. . . .

There was a rustling sound at the window. The light fluctuated briefly—and then a small, glossy leaf blew in through the opening and dropped at her feet.

For a long moment, AMitY stared down at the leaf lying on the dusty floorboards. A tiny drop of moisture—dew or rain or perhaps sap—still quivered at its tip. Wonderingly, she touched the drop with her fingertip, and when the surface tension that held it together was broken, she knew that it was real.

But what did it mean? That the valley was real, too? If the leaf had blown through, then could she also pass from her own world into the one on the other side of the window?

Hesitantly, fearfully, she reached out her hand, prepared to withdraw it quickly should it encounter anything alarming. There was a tingling sensation, a brief chill, and then her hand passed through the opening, unimpeded by the stained glass pane her reason told her was there.

It was cold in the unheated attic, but she felt the warmth of an alien sun on the back of her hand, and the same breeze that had blown the leaf through the window now blew, warm and fragrant, against her face.

She didn't stop to think of danger. As casually as if she was passing through the door of a sonic freshener booth, she rose and climbed through the attic window. Only later would she wonder at her own temerity. For the present, she was concerned with a momentary dizziness, a chill that cut through her body like tiny knives of ice; and then with the problem of easing her feet down on a patch of spongy moss.

When she discovered the ground beneath her was solid, she turned to look back, wanting to be sure that she had a retreat should she need it. Expecting to see the niche under the eaves that she'd just left, she was nonplussed to find that it had disappeared. In its place, a gray mist swirled, filling the opening behind her.

She hesitated briefly before she thrust her hand into the mist. When it disappeared into the grayness and the clammy air of the attic chilled her fingers, she knew that she could return to her own world whenever she chose.

As she started to move away, something glinted at the edge of the opening. She bent closer and saw that a narrow frame surrounded the square of gray mist. In the mellow light it shone with a hard, mirrorlike brilliance; but if it was metal, it was like none she'd ever seen before.

Beneath the opening, a small, crystal dome protruded from the frame. She tried to see inside, but it, too, was filled with a pearly mist. Was it some kind of device to control the portal? She backed away, staring at the great pile of round stones, each the size of a man's torso, that were heaped around the opening, forming a mound above it. Moss covered most of the stones and formed a rich green mortar between; the cairn had an ancient look, as if it had been there for-ever.

She might even have believed it was a natural for-mation if it hadn't been for the oddly formed runes, al-most obliterated by moss, that had been carved into the largest of the stones, this one directly above the mist-filled opening.

For a time, she puzzled over the carvings, won-dering what they meant. They must have been put there by—what? Certainly by beings of intelligence. But if they had a meaning, it was indecipherable to her. Even so, she sensed that the words were a warning, and she felt a sudden chill, the fear she'd been spared until this moment.

Resolutely, she fought against the fear, knowing that she might never get another chance to explore this place, the valley of her dreams; that if she turned back now, she would spend the rest of her life mourning the adventure she'd lost because of her own cowardice.

So she turned her back on the strangely disturbing runes and stood there, her hungry eyes drinking in the wild beauty of the valley.

Although it had been mid-Eleventh month, the first month of winter, on her own world, here the light of E'ewere's sun infused everything with a golden tinge, intensifying the greens, mellowing the grays and browns. The breeze against her face was warm; it was permeated with a delicate fragrance that made her in-hale deeply.

It came to her now that the valley was really an oasis; as far as she could tell, the high cliffs that sur-rounded it were unbroken, isolating it from whatever lay beyond. Perhaps passes cut through that great gray barrier of rock, but none were visible from where she stood. From her vantage point at the narrowest end of the valley, she saw groves of ferny-leaved trees, small fingers of hillocks that ran parallel to the cliffs, an aqua-marine stream that meandered through the meadows below.

For all its lushness, there seemed to be little variety in the trees or the bushes that were scattered here and there on the sloping sides of the valley. At the bottom of the knoll where she stood, a small patch of the blue flowers caught her attention. With only one brief look backward at the cairn of rocks with its metal-framed square of swirling mist, she started down the side of the knoll.

A few minutes later, she was kneeling in a clump of blue-petaled flowers. A delicate scent filled her nostrils, so heady that her head reeled, and she understood now why the breeze was so fragrant.

Although she wanted to sink down into the flow-ers, close her eyes and rest awhile, she shook off her drowsiness and went on. Her robe seemed so cumber-some that she was tempted to take it off and let the sun warm her whole body. After all, there was no one around to be Offended. No buildings, no artifacts, no human sounds. Was she the first of her kind to walk on the spongy moss-grass of this meadow, to pass beneath the outflung branches of this solitary tree, to clamber down this rock-strewn hillside toward the stream that sprang from the head of the valley? One thing was cer-tain: for now, she was alone here in her humanity.

A fever, a delirium rose inside her, so strong that it swept away the last remnants of caution. Again, as she had that time in the O'Zones, she felt an overwhelming urge to run. And run she did—down the valley sloop, past trees so lush they seemed in danger from the weight of their own ferny leaves, past great mounds of the moss-covered rock. She had once read that moss grew only where it was sunless, but here it seemed to thrive everywhere, even directly in the sunlight—or perhaps it wasn't moss at all but some completely alien form of vegetation.

How many other things on E'ewere are not as they seem?

The thought punctured her joy. Suddenly aware of a deep fatigue, she stopped and threw herself down on the grass near a patch of the blue flowers. She stared up at E'ewere's four small moons, just clearing the horizon above the cliffs.

Whoever heard of blue moons, she thought drowsily. *And four blue moons, at that. . . .*

A languor filled her limbs. She closed her eyes and fell asleep to the hum of strange insects, to the distant cry of what sounded like a bird.

How long she slept—a few minutes, an hour—she had no way of knowing. But when she awoke, it was suddenly, as if a voice had called her name. She opened her eyes, and in that first startled moment, she was sure she was still asleep.

A small creature, not more than three feet tall, perched on a rock nearby, watching her. He—surely, a male—was so fragile-looking that she wondered the breeze didn't blow him away. Although human in form, gauzelike wings protruded from his slender back, and his eyes, regarding her with such lively curiosity, were like pools of molten gold.

Again, AMitY felt no fear—maybe because, for all

his alienness, he wasn't totally unfamiliar to her. She had seen others like him in her dreams, caught glimpses of them through the trees, heard snatches of their haunting songs.

The creature moved first. Hesitantly, as if not really sure that she presented no threat, he slid off the rock and, in a graceful half-glide, half-walk, drew closer.

She saw now that a band of gold held back his long, feathery hair, that the green, close-fitting garment he wore, laced from waist to throat, with openings in the back for his wings, was made of a sturdy woven material very much like the sheep's wool she'd seen in museums. Something in the way he stared at her hair, then inspected her rough robe, her belt pouch and seagrass sandals, reminded her of HUmble, and suddenly she was sure that the creature was a very young member of his species.

When he spoke, a trilling sound that was meaningless to her, AMitY shook her head. "I don't un'stand you. Do you speak my language?"

The creature came near enough to reach out his hand and touch her forehead. She felt a tingling inside her head. Only the realization that he couldn't be expected to observe the Courtesies kept her from pulling away with a hiss of Offense.

With a nod, as if answering some question of his own, he stepped back finally. "You are not a Golden Barb," he said with such relief that she wondered where he'd found the courage to come so close.

"My name is AMitY. I'm a citizen of—of a world called Earth," she said, too curious to feel shy. "What —*who* are you?"

"I am Dl'lark, Prince of the A'aludes." He placed both hands on his chest and bowed deeply from the waist. Although the bow was respectful, the fluttering of his wings gave away his excitement, and again, AMitY was sure he was very young. "The pass through the mountains is open again?" he added.

"I didn't come through a pass. I came through—" She stopped because she didn't know what word to use. Door? Gateway? Surely, she couldn't call it a window.

But she didn't have to explain. Dl'lark gave a dismayed look toward the cairn at the end of the valley. His wings rippled so violently that she was afraid he'd lose his balance.

"You came through the Portal?" he said, his voice hushed.

"You call it a portal?"

"It *is* the Portal. What else would we call it?"

"Did your people put it there?"

"It was there when we first came to the valley. This was my day to guard the Portal but"—he gave her a sheepish smile—"a flock of gellums flew overhead. I followed them, hoping one would drop a black feather for my mother's hair." He paused, and again his eyes were bright with curiosity. "This Earth of yours—is it like E'ewere?"

"No, it's ver' dif'rent—at least, where I live. There are few trees or other plants. Only build'n's and streets and—and lots of cit'zens."

"Is it beautiful?"

"Not any more. I think it must have been a lot like this valley a long time ago."

Unconsciously, she sighed, and Dl'lark's face clouded. He gave a half-hop toward her, his amber eyes full of sympathy. "Do not be sad, My Lady AMitY. Be glad that the Portal chose you. It is a great honor." Before she could ask what he meant, he added, "Until I saw your hair, I thought you were the Troggo—and then I was afraid you were a Golden Barb."

"The Troggo? Who is that?"

"He is our enemy." He shuddered so violently that his wings fluttered open.

So even these gentle people had their problems, AMitY thought, aware of disappointment. And from Dl'lark's agitation, their enemies must be very dangerous indeed.

"What does the Troggo look like?" she asked.

"No one knows, not even Lord Som'mos, our Keeper of Legends. It has been a hundred times a hundred sun-cycles since the Old One gave us the task of guarding the Portal, and many of the old legends have been lost. But always we watch for our enemy, the Troggo. If he finds his way through the Portal, then we must hide in the caves as we do when the Golden Barb come through the pass—and one of us must go to the Old One, who lives beyond the desert, to tell him that E'ewere has been"—he paused as if searching for a word—"invaded."

"And today was your turn to watch?"

"Yes. It is a very great responsibility. My father will be unhappy because I failed in my duty."

He looked so forlorn that AMitY had to hide a smile. More than ever, he reminded her of HUmble—and how she wished her young brother could be here with her! How he would glory in exploring this world he knew only from dreams. . . .

"Do not be sad, My Lady," Dl'lark said softly.

AMitY smiled at him. "I'm not sad. In fact, I'm very happy to be here."

Dl'lark's face brightened. "Sad is hurtful, but happy feels very good."

She couldn't help laughing, this time at his mecurial change of mood. "How is it that you speak English?" she asked curiously.

"English? What is English?"

"My language. You spoke something else at first."

"That was the speak-aloud of the Golden Barb. 'Are you a Golden Barb?' I asked. It is polite to use the—the language of a visitor, even if they are enemies. I found yours in—" He touched her forehead again.

As the significance of his words sank in, AMitY felt such a strong revulsion that she flinched away from him. Dl'lark's small body reeled; his eyes turned dull and his wings collapsed around him like a pile of discarded gauze. Alarmed, AMitY caught his almost weightless body before it could reach the ground, then stood there, holding him in her arms, not knowing how to help him.

Slowly, Dl'lark's eyes cleared and his lavender-and-gold wings resumed their erect position. When she sat him back on his feet, he looked at her strangely, as if he were afraid of her.

"Are you ill?" she asked anxiously.

"It was your anger, My Lady AMitY. It hurt me—inside." He touched his own forehead. "Why were you so angry with me?"

"It was the shock of learn'n that you could—" She bogged down, not knowing what to call it. "That you could hear my thoughts. I didn't know such a th'n was pos'ble."

"Your kind does not mind-speak?"

"No. We don't b'lieve in such th'n's."

"But that is sad! To be so alone is very sad."

He looked so distressed that AMitY decided it was time to change the subject before his wings began to droop again. "Your people—they call themselves A'aludes?"

"Our legends say that long ago we had a different name. We were driven from the world of our origin when our sun grew cold; then we were driven from our first place of refuge, our second home, by the Troggo. When we were given refuge in E'ewere, which is our third home, the Old One told us we must forget the past and learn new ways, so he gave us a new name. In our speak-aloud, *a'alude* is the word for peace." He stared at her fixedly. "And the name for your kind—are you called Citizens?"

AMitY thought a moment, trying to decide among several words: *human beings, earthlings, mankind. . . .*

"We are people," she said finally.

She jumped when Dl'lark's small body began to shake, when a high-pitched sound emerged from his throat. At first, she thought she'd frightened him again, and then she realized he was laughing.

"Why are you laughing?" she asked crossly.

"But *we* are people," he said when he could talk again. "So how could *you* be, too?" He wiped his eyes on his sleeve. "Lord Som'mos will have many legends to tell about your visit. And my mother will sing a special song for you."

"Is your mother a singer?"

"We are all singers. But she is the best." His eyes danced with mischief suddenly. "Wocho will be sorry now that he didn't keep me company today. He had no duties because he has just worked eight days in the peat bogs. He promised to stand watch with me, but then he decided he'd rather hunt for sunstones instead."

"Who is Wocho?"

"He is—" He paused, his eyes unfocussed, and briefly, AMitY felt a tingling sensation inside her head. "You do not have such a word. You would call Lord Wocho my ménage-mate."

"Is ev'body here on E'ewere a lord or lady—or a prince?"

"Of course. Is it different on your world?"

"Well, we do have a few princes in N'York State," she said dryly, thinking of ConCord, who, in his own way, was royalty. "Most of us are just or'nary cit'zens."

"Does this not cause sadness? To set a few above the rest, I mean?"

"We are taught to 'cept the wisdom of the Code," she said. When Dl'lark was silent, she added, "Surely, you must live by laws of some kind?"

"We follow the teachings of the Old One—and then there are the legends." Dl'lark gave a deep sigh. "Every year at Harvest Gathering, Lord Som'mos, who is Keeper of Legends as well as our teacher, recites the oldest ones. They are very long." He made a droll face. "I usually fall asleep—unless someone sees me and gives me a mind-twitch."

"What's that?"

"Like you just did." He rubbed his head. "It was very hurtful."

"I'm sorry. I was startled 'cause it would be 'sidered a 'trusion 'mong my people to—to read their thoughts."

Dl'lark's luminous eyes regarded her with such pity that she added hurriedly, "Your parents—will they be 'fraid of me?'"

"Oh, they know you mean us no harm."

She puzzled over this ambiguous statement for a moment, then asked, "You spoke of the Golden Barb—do they come here often?"

Although she was getting used to Dl'lark's swift changes of mood, she was alarmed when his wings twitched violently. "Do not fear, My Lady. Others keep watch for them. There will be plenty of warning."

"Do they come through the mountain pass?"

"Yes—but it has been closed off by rock slides for a long time now." He paused to shake his head. "We hide in the caves when they come, and after they take all the food and gold they can carry, they go away again. But sometimes they find our caves and then they—they remove our wings and take us off to be their slaves. They are strong, much larger even than you. It is said their hair is the color of fire, which is why I thought at first you might be one."

He fluttered closer. Delicately, he stroked her hair. Although AMitY was shocked by his boldness, she held herself still, not wanting to Offend. Never before in her life had anyone, not even her mother, taken such a liberty with her. She felt repelled and yet—and yet there was something comforting about Dl'lark's gently stroking hand, too. Was this more proof of her depravity? If so, it seemed a harmless deviation from the normal. . . .

Dl'lark's hand dropped away. "My mother will sing many songs about you. There is a legend that someday a being with hair of fire and eyes the same color as Our Lord Tok'ko"—he gestured toward the stream below—"will save us from a great danger. And I will be in the legend Lord Som'mos tells about you. Many life-cycles from now, others will know that it was Prince Dl'lark who found you and became your first friend. And then Wocho will really be sorry that he changed his mind today."

He sounded so smug that AMitY had to smile. "Will your father punish you for leaving your post?" she asked.

The corners of Dl'lark's mouth drooped. "He will make me work extra days in the peat bogs—or maybe in the mines. He knows I hate the mines because they are so dark and musty."

"Maybe it will make a dif'rence when you tell him that you were d'verted by—what did you call them? Gellums?— 'cause you wanted to get a feather for your mother's hair."

"Or maybe he will be so busy making preparations for the gathering in your honor that he will forget about me." He seemed cheered by the prospect.

"How long will it take us to get there? I'm eager to meet your parents."

"My mother, Queen Aur'ri, and others of the welcoming party will be here soon. They would have come at once, but first they had to change their clothes for the gathering in your honor."

"I don't un'stand—did you signal them with some sort of commun'cation device?"

"Device? I do not know that word."

"It is a—a mech'nism made of metal." At his blank look, she added, "You mentioned gold so you must know what metal is. In our world, we have a device that sends messages from one quad to another through the air—" She stopped because Dl'lark was doubled over again, emitting the high-pitched sound she knew was laughter.

She waited until his paroxysm of mirth was over and he was wiping his eyes before she said, a little waspishly, "Haven't you ev' heard of anyth'n like that?"

"But we have no need for such things! And gold is for making body ornaments, for spinning into thread to decorate our gathering clothes or to mold into beautiful things that pleasure our eyes. What a strange world you come from, almost as strange as that of the Golden Barb." The laughter left his eyes suddenly. "It is said that they are so barbaric that they eat the bodies of other creatures. Surely, your kind doesn't practice such savagery?"

AMitY remembered, a little guiltily, the fish broth she'd had for thirdmeal that day. "At one time," she said evasively, "we did raise cattle and other an'mals for such purposes, but no longer. And you haven't 'splained how your parents know 'bout me."

"I used mind-speak, of course. How else would we warn each other when the Gra'ack is overhead?"

"Gra'ack?" She said the strange, clacking word gingerly.

Dl'lark shuddered so violently that for a moment, she thought his filigreed headband would fall off. "The Gra'ack came through the Portal many life-cycles ago and now it preys upon us and the animals of the valley. Since it came from another world—perhaps it was your Earth?"

"What does it look like?"

"It is black—black as the peat in the bogs at the other end of the valley. And its claws are sharp, its wings strong enough to carry off even our largest male—"

He broke off, his head tilted to one side. "The welcoming party comes now. I have already told them that mind-speak offends you. Do not fear that they will intrude."

He turned and pointed upward, and it seemed to AMitY, in that first bewildering moment, that she had been inundated by a bevy of purple-and-gold butterflies, by a chorus of chiming bells, by a dozen pair of luminous, golden eyes.

ater, AMitY would get to know the A'aludes who came to greet her very well. She would learn that their personalities—from pompous Lord Som'mos, the Keeper of Legends, to Wocho, Dl'lark's shy friend—were as varied as their wings of orchid, lavender, plum—and all the shades between. But for now, she was overwhelmed by the profusion of swirling wings and graceful, reedlike bodies, of eyes the color of E'ewere's sun, of voices like chiming cymbals.

As her stunned eyes took in their pastel garments, woven from some supple, silky material and embroidered with gold thread, she realized that the ornaments that gleamed on their fingers and wrists were also gold. It was difficult to reconcile this evidence of vast wealth with the impression she'd received from Dl'lark that his people were simple farmers and miners, living a quiet life in their isolated valley.

At first, only one stood out from the rest, perhaps because she stood apart from the others, her eyes warm, her lips curved into a welcoming smile. AMitY didn't need to see the delicate gold-filigree band that bound her pale hair to know that she was Dl'lark's mother. Although it seemed odd to think of a being only three feet tall as regal, this was the word that came into AMitY's mind. As she smiled back shyly, she discovered that her bewilderment had evaporated, replaced by a sense of well-being.

"I am Aur'ri, Queen of the A'aludes." The small creature's voice was lilting, bell-like in its clarity. "Welcome to E'ewere, young traveler. Our son"—she leveled a long look at Dl'lark, who promptly tried to lose himself behind a rather stout male with plum-colored wings—"tells us that you came through the Portal from a place called Earth. Since your kind does not practice mind-talk, be assured that we will not intrude upon your inner thoughts."

A twittering arose from the others. She stilled it with a gesture of her diminutive hand, then pointed to the four blue moons on the horizon. "Tonight, when Our Lord Luk'ko and his three sisters are directly overhead, we will celebrate your coming with a gathering. But first, you must rest, enjoy some"—she paused and briefly AMitY felt the now-familiar tingling inside her head—"tea-treat."

She must have caught AMitY's instinctive flinch because her eyes dimmed briefly. "I did not intrude, My Lady AMitY. I touched only that small part of your inner self that deals with what you call language and we call speak-aloud. My son, before he knew that you were different, plucked a few words from your mind. It is a language we are already familiar with, having learned an earlier form of it many sun-cycles ago. You speak it differently, but then—in time—all languages change with the cycles."

"I'm not the first from Earth to visit you?" AMitY asked eagerly.

"Many sun-cycles ago, one of your kind came through the Portal, seeking refuge. He had been wounded in one of your wars, and when he was well again, he returned to his own world. He was a kindly man who taught us much. We urged him to stay, to finish his life-cycle with us, but he had a task yet unfinished—a quest, he called it."

Queen Aur'ri sighed deeply. "We have many songs and legends about him. Like you, he pleased the eye. It is said that all our maidens cried when he returned to his own world."

She turned to look up at the cairn on the knoll above them. "It was he who carved the message into the stone above the Portal, reminding us always to remain on guard against our enemy, the Troggo."

Her face was so grave that AMitY felt a sudden chill—and a stir of curiosity. Before she could speak, Queen Aur'ri, in one of the quick changes of mood AMitY had noticed in her son, clapped her hands together, her smile radiant again. "Come, this is not the time to speak of enemies, not when we have a new friend to honor. We will take you to the village now."

She slipped her hand into AMitY's; it felt as unsubstantial as a rainbow. AMitY was so afraid she might crush those fragile fingers that it wasn't until later she realized she'd felt no revulsion at the small alien's touch.

It was a long walk, even for someone used to daily hour-long treks to and from the Ed-Complex. But with Queen Aur'ri to point out things of interest—a grove of trees that bore pale green fruit, a patch of water plants she called "alissa," a cave set into the cliffs where goldsmiths worked the precious metal that came from the valley's gold mines—it seemed no time at all before they came to the first dwelling.

The roof of the tiny cottage was thatched with saffron-colored dried grass, and the ever-present moss covered its stone walls so that it seemed to blend into its surroundings as if it had grown there. Despite its charm, it looked very primitive, even to AMitY's inexperienced eyes, at odds with the silken raiments and gold ornaments of the welcoming party.

Was there a strong caste system here, after all, she wondered, again aware of a feeling of disquiet. Somehow, from her conversation with Dl'lark, she had gotten the impression that there were few class distinctions among the A'aludes.

Queen Aur'ri must have noticed her troubled face because she asked, "What is it? Do you see something that displeases you, My Lady AMitY?"

"I was wondering—is this the home of one of your"—AMitY groped for the word—"your peasants?"

"Peasant? This word is not familiar to me."

"A—a farmer is a better word," AMitY said hastily.

"Ah . . . but we are all farmers here. Each of us, except the tradesmen and the draftsmen and the very young, work their allotted hours in the fields." She shook her head sadly. "As it is, we barely stay ahead of the chuk'ki."

"Chuk'ki?"

In answer, Queen Aur'ri tapped her small foot on the emerald-green moss they were standing on. "It grows so fast—always we fight to keep it from smothering our fields."

"But it's so beautiful," AMitY protested.

"Yes, it *is* beautiful, and we destroy only what encroaches upon the fields allotted us by the Old One." Queen Aur'ri smiled suddenly. "Look—young Lord Tur'ri is watching us from the window, too shy to come out to greet you."

Through a recessed window of the cottage, a child was peeking out at them. When he waved timidly, AMitY waved back, not at all surprised that he was intimidated at what must seem a giant to him.

What was it her grandfather had said when she'd described the A'aludes? That such fragile creatures couldn't possibly survive unless they had no natural enemies? That without such enemies, their food needs would soon outstrip their supplies?

But it seemed that neither thing had happened to the A'aludes. So how explain their survival? Perhaps the raids of the Golden Barb—and the Gra'ack—kept down their numbers. Did they prosper only because their enemies hadn't found a way into the valley in recent years?

As they went on, AMitY realized that she'd lost some of her first awe of the A'aludes. Now she noticed that despite their fine garments and their gold ornaments, their hands, even the Queen's, showed signs of hard work. What a paradox these small creatures were, she thought; and how she wished her grandfather was here to decipher them for her!

As if Queen Aur'ri sensed AMitY's preoccupation with her own thoughts, she was silent now, and it was a quiet group that finally reached the village.

AMitY looked around with undisguised curiosity. Encircling a small meadow were several tiny shops. Around it, scattered throughout groves of tall trees, were dozens of moss-covered stone cottages, the door of each dwelling tinted a different color. There were no paths between the cottages, and for the first time, it occurred to AMitY that what had been a longish trek for her must have been a real trial to her winged hosts.

In consternation, she stared at the Queen's delicate slippers. Of course! Why would aerial creatures have need for sturdy shoes?

Before she could put her concern into words, she was engulfed by a fresh wave of greeters. Although she didn't doubt the sincerity of the A'aludes' welcome, she was sure now that she read pity in their golden eyes.

Was it because of her clumsiness, her size—or because of her clothes, so rough and ugly among such finery? To her bemused eyes, it seemed that everybody, from the smallest child to the queen, seemed equally well-clad in their shimmering garments, with gold bands encircling their fingers and waists, and strands of the precious metal plaited through their long hair. The puzzle she was determined to solve was: how could a people as simple as the A'aludes possibly possess such riches?

The building she was taken to, which Queen Aur'ri called their guest dwelling, was much larger than the other cottages she'd seen. It sat alone in the midst of the trees, and although the structure was in good repair, it had a neglected look, as if it were seldom used.

"How often do strangers come through the Portal?" she asked Queen Aur'ri, who, along with the other members of the welcoming party, had accompanied her through the pathless woods to the guest dwelling.

"You are the first since the Gra'ack found its way here five life-cycles ago." For a moment, there was sadness on the Queen's serene face, but it quickly changed to a smile. "And this is not the time to speak of the Gra'ack. Now you must rest and refresh yourself. Already the weavers are working on your bedcovers. My daughter, Princess Gw'wanna, is supervising the making of a garment for you to wear to the gathering in your honor. The musicians are tuning up their instruments and the dancers—oh, they have such a splendid dance planned to entertain you, My Lady AMitY! My lifemate, King L'lando, who was helping with the legume harvesting when Dl'lark's call came, is hurrying back from the lower valley at this moment. He will welcome you properly at the gathering."

"Please . . . don't go to any special trouble for me. I'm not really a lady, you know. I'm just an ord'nary cit'zen."

"But you are not at all ordinary! And besides"—Queen Aur'ri's eyes twinkled at AMitY—"we A'aludes are always happy for an excuse for a gathering. It has been a long time since anyone from the outside has come to the valley."

"Not even through the pass?"

She had addressed the question to Queen Aur'ri, but it was Lord Som'mos, looking dignified and very important in a pale green tunic and rather snug trousers, who stepped forward to answer her.

"You are our first visitor since the Great Storm." His voice was deep, surprisingly resonant for such a small creature. When he paused and cast his eyes upward as if rehearsing his next words, AMitY caught the look of dismay on Dl'lark's face and had to hide a smile.

"It was during the second sun-cycle of King L'lando's reign that the Great Storm devastated our valley," Lord Som'mos entoned. "Just before harvest that year, rain and wind and hail the size of brook-stones lashed the fields, destroying the grain and legumes, drowning out the water plants, casting down the fruit that was ripening on the trees. When it was over, the only food was wild herbs from the upper valleys, nuts from the tuk'ku trees, and milk and cheese from those of our animals who had not been swept away in the flood that ravished the valley.

"That year, many of our elders chose to go into the Wild Wood so there would be food for the young. During the storm, which lasted three nights and two days, torrents of water poured down the cliffs, eroding them and sending tons of stones into the pass, filling it with debris. Since then, no one has come here from the outside, not even the trinket peddler with his pack. Of course, even before the storm, few visited us here. At one time, a messenger came once every few sun-cycles from the Old One, inquiring if all were well with us. But since the storm, this one has not come."

"But surely you don't need the pass. Couldn't you fly over the mountains?"

Lord Som'mos's plum-colored wings twitched so hard they almost unfurled. "We are forbidden to leave the valley," he said quickly, looking alarmed.

Queen Aur'ri touched AMitY's hand. "Lord Som'mos will tell you more of this another time. He will have many questions to ask you about this Earth of yours." She turned and beckoned to two of the women who had accompanied them. "This is Lady Gl'loro and Lady Dom'mi. They will make you comfortable and bring tea-treat to refresh you."

Before AMitY could say again that she didn't want to be a bother, Queen Aur'ri had bowed and was fluttering away through the trees, and AMitY's two attendants were gently urging her toward the guest house.

Although she had to bend her head to get through the door, the ceiling of the room inside was high enough that she could stand erect, making her wonder at the size of the—what had Lord Som'mos called him? The trinket peddlar?—and the messenger from the Old One, who seemed to be some kind of guardian to the A'aludes.

A few minutes later, she was sitting cross-legged on a large floor cushion, drinking something sweet and cool and delicious from a gold tankard. She admired the delicate pattern of flowers etched on the handle of the vessel, then looked around wide-eyed at the tapestry wall hangings, the richly colored rugs on the stone floor. Although the only furniture was one small table of darkly grained wood and a chest with an intricately carved front, there were several piles of the brightly colored cushions, made of the same silky material as her attendants' clothing.

The two women withdrew, murmuring softly that she must rest. After they were gone, AMitY finished her drink and sank into a mound of cushions, intending to rest her eyes while she thought over the things she'd seen and heard and sorted them out in her mind.

A moment later, she was asleep.

he amber light of day was gone when AMitY awoke. The room was filled with a silvery blueness that she remembered from her dreams, and she knew that the four blue moons of E'ewere must be directly overhead. What had Queen Aur'ri called them? Our Lord Luk'ko and his three sisters? How strange that the A'aludes seemed to have noble names for everything, including their moons, their brook—and their guests.

A light flickered into life nearby. AMitY sat up quickly and saw that a young female had entered the room, carrying a boat-shaped lamp. With her delicate features, willowy figure, and the orchid wings that were tightly furled at her back, the A'alude girl was very lovely. Her pale green gown fell in soft folds from her shoulders to her knees, and a chain of gold links encircled her supple waist. The coronet on her head looked very fragile, as if a breath of wind would break its tiny strands of gold filigree.

When she saw that AMitY was awake, she gave a low bow. "I am Princess Gw'wanna," she said, sounding a little shy. She displayed a gown of soft blue, embroidered with the same gold thread that enhanced her own gown. "This is your garment for the gathering tonight. Tomorrow, sturdier clothing will be prepared for you for everyday wear."

"It's beau'ful," AMitY said, a little awed. She stroked the delicate fabric with her fingertips. "I've only seen such mater'als in museums. Is it silk?"

Gw'wanna hesitated, as if searching through her memory. "It is much like your silk, I believe. Our Lady Sab'bri spins it for us. She provides thread for our looms, and in return, we give her comfort and companionship."

The small princess produced a pair of slippers; although they were made of the same material as the gown, they were dark blue, more utilitarian than the gown. "Tomorrow, Lord Tur'ru, the slippermaker, will measure your feet for a better fit." She smiled, showing a deep dimple in each cheek. "These were made for Lord Top'po, the dyer, who has the largest feet in the valley."

As she went on to describe the celebration to come, she began untying the leather belt around AMitY's waist. Rather than Offend by pulling away, AMitY permitted the liberty—and then found that she didn't really mind, after all, not even when Gw'wanna gently pulled her robe off over her head.

Gw'wanna touched AMitY's shoulder blade. "But there are no scars," she said wonderingly.

"Scars?"

"Where your wings were—severed."

It took a moment, but suddenly AMitY understood the pity she'd sensed earlier. "My people have no wings," she said gently.

"Ah . . . I am so glad that you are not maimed! We

knew, of course, that others, like the trinket peddler, do not possess the gift of flight." The brief radiance of her smile faded. "But how do you reach high places, My Lady? How do you gather herbs from the cliff crevices and fruit from the top of the tree where it grows the sweetest?"

"We walk and climb and sometimes use ladders and other devices. Not nearly as convenient as wings, but we manage," AMitY said dryly.

Gw'wanna nodded her understanding. "Like the Golden Barbs. They too are bound to the earth." She hesitated, then asked deferentially, "You are young like me?"

"I reached maturity a few weeks ago."

"Then we are the same age. Already I have been feted at the woman-rites, and now I am old enough for—what do your people call it? Mating?"

"Bond'n—or, if it's not for life, we call it pair'n. Do you have—someone special?"

"Oh, yes. I am promised to Lord Tor'ro."

AMitY smiled, remembering the name as belonging to one of the welcoming party, a tall young male with wings that dwarfed the others.

"He is ver' handsome," she said aloud.

A faint tinge of rose invaded Gw'wanna's ivory cheeks, but AMitY was sure she saw sadness in the girl's eyes as she asked, "And you, My Lady? Has someone won your heart?"

Unbidden, an image of ConCord slipped into AMitY's mind, but she suppressed it and said firmly, "There is no one special." To change the subject, she added, "Ev'body speaks my language so well here. At first, it was dif'cult to un'stand your brother, but he seemed to 'prove as we talked. And when the others came, they spoke as well as I do 'though they use the formal mode, the one we 'serve for books."

Gw'wanna looked puzzled. "Why does that surprise you? What one of us knows, all know—unless it is intimate knowledge and therefore protected. Dl'lark probed your mind while you slept among the dream flowers on the hillside—" She broke off and popped both hands over her mouth. "I was not to speak of this because so many things cause offense to your kind!"

AMitY regarded her in silence. *Was* she Offended because Dl'lark had entered her mind while she slept? This was the ultimate invasion of privacy, a violation of her innermost Place of Being—so why didn't she feel shocked? Was she truly a Deviate—or was it simply because it was impossible to resent anything these creatures, so obviously well-meaning, did?

A few minutes later, AMitY sat quietly as Gw'wanna brushed out her hair, then plaited it with strands of the fine gold chain. Ignoring AMitY's protests, she transferred one of her own gleaming bracelets to AMitY's wrist before she handed her a small hand mirror.

Fascinated by the first clear image she'd ever seen of her own face, AMitY stared into the mirror. Was *this* how she appeared to other citizens? This girl with her vivid hair and eyes, her skin that looked as if she'd just spent a day in the Parklands? No wonder she was regarded with so much suspicion. . . .

"Do you not like your gown?" Gw'wanna asked her anxiously.

"It's a beau'ful gown. It's just that—well, this is the first time I've ever seen my own r'flection."

"There are no mirrors on your world?"

"My people c'sider it vain to look at one's own image. And Vanity is one of the Twenty Sins 'gainst Order."

Gw'wanna's laugh was like bubbling brook water. "But it is so pleasant to look into the mirror when one is young and pleasing to the eye! What is wrong with such an innocent pleasure?"

Since AMitY didn't have an answer to that, at least one that would make sense to Gw'wanna, she was glad when the princess took her hand and led her through the door, out into the blue-tinged evening.

Others joined them as they strolled through the woods to the circle of grassy meadow in the middle of the village. The air hummed with the sound of voices, the flurrying of wings, the tuning of musical instruments, the clatter of wooden plates and bowls. Woven mats had been arranged at one end of the meadow to hold the food for the celebration, and from the pungent odors that filled the air, from glimpses AMitY caught of the mounds of the same pale green fruit she'd seen earlier, of flat, brown loaves of bread, of steaming bowls of what she guessed were vegetables, she knew that while she'd been asleep, others had been busy preparing a feast in her honor.

Queen Aur'ri, regal in a flowing white gown, came to greet her. The tall male beside her, who wore a purple robe that matched his magnificant span of wings, was King L'lando. As AMitY returned his bow, she wasn't surprised that Dl'lark, hovering nearby, had a dejected look, and she suspected he'd already been chastised by his father.

The king indicated that AMitY was to occupy the seat of honor at his right hand. As gracefully as she could manage, she sank down onto a large cushion, wondering if she looked as huge and awkward as she felt, looming above even King L'lando, the tallest of the A'alude males.

With a clap of her hands, Queen Aur'ri signalled the feasting to begin. A few minutes later, when AMitY took her first bite of the food in front of her, she couldn't help thinking of HUmble, whose appetite had been the despair of their parents and the cause of numerous lectures on the Sin of Gluttony.

Besides the green fruit and the crusty bread, which had been spread with a succulent yellow-colored substance, there were purple berries, plump and glistening, and an assortment of cooked vegetables and herbs, washed down with more of the heady liquid the A'aludes politely called tea-treat although it bore no resemblance to the pallid drink of her own world.

The finishing touch of the meal were tiny berry-filled tarts, so tender that they seemed to melt on the tongue, and now it was PRudenCe, with her weakness for sweets, that AMitY found herself thinking of.

The entertainment began. As AMitY watched the dancers, whirling and tumbling through the air, their colored garments and the rich purples of their wings forming a rainbow of colors, she felt a deep sadness that she couldn't share this feast of the senses with her loved ones.

Perhaps Queen Aur'ri caught her sadness, because when the dancing was over and she rose, her face was grave, unsmiling.

One of the older musicians, his oddly shaped instrument strung with silvery threads, settled down near her feet, and the murmuring of the celebrants ceased. The musician's agile fingers began plucking out a melodious tune, and the Queen's voice filled AMitY's head, touching her innermost being.

"I sing a song this special day,
To welcome you, Gentle Stranger,
To our land—E'ewere.

From memory and legend, we learned fear,
Guard the Portal.
Keep the Watch always.
Beware.
Protect this valley;
Green coolness and flower-scented air.
Guard the Portal.
Keep the watch.
Beware.

But from you, My Lady AMitY, we sense no danger.
In your eyes, love's golden light
Burns constant and bright.

With trusting hearts and extended hands,
We welcome you, Gentle Stranger,
To E'ewere, our land."

As the last strains of the haunting melody died away, as the words of welcome, of trust, echoed through her mind, AMitY was filled with an irrational nostalgia, not for her own world, but for E'ewere, as if she were already saying goodbye.

I must remember every moment of this, she thought, and found that her cheeks were wet with tears.

fter three days, AMitY, immersed in her new life, sometimes found it hard to remember the Earth. How could that gray, static world compare to a place where there was something new to observe, to learn, every waking minute of the day?

Although Queen Aur'ri told AMitY that their climate was not always so benign as it was during this, their harvest season, she found it hard to believe that the valley was subject to storms and droughts, periods of hot, humid weather and even an occasional cold spell that froze the water at the edge of Our Lord Tok'ko.

There was so much to learn about the valley, even about such mundane things as how to cope with the peat fires that the A'aludes burned in their stone fireplaces.

To save precious fuel (and, AMitY suspected, to provide themselves with companionship) the A'alude women shared their cooking chores, with three or four families eating their meals together on a rotating basis. Since the oily peat they used for both cooking and heat was very smoky and irritating to the eyes, she was doubly grateful that it was harvest season, that the thick stone walls of the cottages retained enough of the day's warmth after the sun had gone down so that a fire was seldom necessary.

As the villagers went about their everyday duties and chores, dressed in their serviceable garments of homespun wool, it was easier for her to accept the truth—that despite the gold ornaments and the richly embroidered finery they wore at their gatherings, the A'aludes lived simple, almost primitive lives. Although they slept on soft floor cushions and drank from the gold tankards that were individually cast for each child as he approached his first birthday, they had no concept of even the most rudimentary technology.

That they could remain so cheerful as they went about their chores, AMitY could only attribute to a natural optimism that she wished she possessed. But then, she reminded herself, she hadn't been able to accept the Disciplines, so how could she help thinking that the A'alude's philosophy of refusing to speak of anything sad, of banishing worry by simply not thinking about it, was very dangerous?

From the first day, she observed that everybody, including the members of the royal family, did his or her share of the work, whether it was cooking or gathering fruit, working in the food drying yard or caring for the domestic animals. Queen Aur'ri and Gw'wanna helped with the community cooking, kept their own snug cottage tidy, and once a week, they joined the other women of the village at a long, stone building built over a warm spring, there to do the family washing.

Along with all able-bodied A'alude males older than ten sun-cycles, King L'lando took his turn in the fields, in the peat bogs and mines—and at the guard stations where a constant watch was kept. One station was located at the Portal, another on a high ledge that overlooked the pass, while at each end of the valley a constant watch was kept for the Gra'ack. The A'aludes's fear of this sky-borne menace was brought home to AMitY when she realized that of all the creatures they mentioned, the Gra'ack, the barbaric Golden Barbs and the Troggo were the only ones not given a respectful title.

Dl'lark had been appointed to be AMitY's guide, but it was usually in the company of two or more others—sometimes children, sometimes young adults—that she was shown the wonders of the valley.

In the large stone building set aside for this purpose, she met the village weavers, who showed her how they loomed cloth for garments, bedding, wall hangings and rugs, not only from the wool thread that came from the fleece of their sheeplike domestic animals, but from the silk thread spun for them by the guest they called Our Lady Sab'bri.

At large wooden vats, she watched as the cloth was tinted half a dozen colors by dyes made from flowers and crushed leaves of plants, from bark and the clays of the valley. The garments that were made from the cloth by the village sewers and embroiderers were available to all who needed them, including AMitY, who secretly thought she looked very dashing in her green everyday tunic, close-fitting trousers and matching sandals, with wooden soles that the slippermaster had made especially sturdy for her earthbound feet.

In a deep cave, lighted by the goldsmiths' fiery forge, she spent an afternoon watching the goldmaster at work, fascinated by the dexterity of his skillful fingers as he cast the precious metal into a goblet for a recently weaned child. His apprentices were entrusted with the simpler task of spinning molten gold into thread to decorate a new gathering gown for the woodcarver's wife.

AMitY visited the slippermaker and the woodcarver in their cluttered shops, the bakery where the villagers' bread and succulent fruit- and berry-tarts were baked. In the stone spring house where milk from the A'alude's goatlike dairy animals was stored, she took a turn at one of the wooden churns that produced the yellow spread for their bread that, when aged, became a mellow food that was one of the staples of the A'alude diet.

With Dl'lark as her guide, she explored the fruit orchards where each tree had its own name and was treated as if it were an old friend. Although their simple tools, as well as the stools and chests and tables that furnished their cottages, were made of wood, it was only, Dl'lark told her, after some natural catastrophe or old age had felled a tree that its wood was utilized. AMitY finally understood why the cottages were so sparsely furnished, and why the A'aludes burned the smoky, inefficient peat rather than wood for their cooking.

The fields, too, where the grains and vegetables and legumes grew, were treated with deep respect. AMitY already knew the A'alude were vegetarians; it didn't take her long to discover that their concern for life extended to the wild creatures who shared the valley with them. They might shoo away a pesky gellums, one of the quarrelsome black birds that sometimes descended upon the fields in droves, but when AMitY suggested they put out traps, Lord Chu'uko, the fieldmaster, looked shocked and told her that the Old One had forbidden them to enslave their friends, the birds, who had as much claim to freedom as they did.

At the invitation of Lord Som'mos, who was the village teacher as well as the Keeper of Legends, she joined a circle of children in the village round. As she listened to their trilling voices while they recited oral history and sang traditional songs in her honor, she wondered why such gifted people had no written language. Was it because of their mind-talk that they'd never felt the need to develop writing?

During a session with Lord Som'mos, it was AMitY's turn to answer questions about herself and her own world. As Keeper of Legends, he told her, it was his duty to compose a new legend about her, one that would be passed down to his successor. While AMitY was flattered to learn that her visit would be known to generations of yet-unborn A'aludes, she was uncomfortably aware how dreary her world must seem to these people—and also very comical, if she could judge from Dl'lark's reaction to some of the Litanies.

Once, when she described the strict rule against baymates becoming friends, she caught a smile even on Lord Som'mos's somber face, as if he couldn't quite believe such nonsense. While AMitY had always chaffed at the ban, to her surprise she found herself wanting to defend it, to explain that if friendships were permitted among baymates, then inevitably there would be whispering in the bays—and that would disturb those who were trying to sleep.

But she held her tongue, knowing that it would be impossible to explain to these people, who were constantly touching each other, who groomed each other's hair and seemed never to do anything alone by choice, that in her overcrowded world every irritant that might make life intolerable must be eliminated lest it break down the rigid structure of society.

"Do your legends tell you who constructed the Portal?" she asked Lord Som'mos after she had become convinced that the A'aludes could never have possessed the technology necessary to construct a matter transmitter.

"It has always been here," he said, shrugging. "Its history is unknown to us."

"And yet—your people came here through the Portal," she said thoughtfully.

"From the world where we'd taken refuge after the sun of our homeworld died—or so our oldest legend says." He sighed deeply. "Our second home was as fair as E'ewere—until the Troggo came. He invaded our lands, cut down our sacred trees to use for fuel and to build his dwelling place. He robbed us of our food and treasure and killed those of us he captured. For many life-cycles, those who survived went into hiding, but it was a very dangerous life because of the Troggo's great mind-power and physical strength.

"Then the Portal summoned one of our kind, a Prince of the royal blood. His name was Luk'ko—we named E'ewere's largest moon in his honor. He traveled far on this world and had many adventures, looking for a refuge for his people. Eventually, he found the citadel of the Old One, who took pity upon our plight and gave Prince Luk'ko permission to lead his people through the Portal and into the valley. Our Honored Ancestor returned for his three sisters and for those others of his people who still survived. One by one, he brought them here, into this sweet land.

"Since then, we have obeyed the rules the Old One laid down for us—and always, we guard the Portal, watching for the Troggo, lest he find us again."

"But this all happened such a long time ago, Lord Som'mos," AMitY said. "Surely the Troggo has been dead for thousands of years now."

"There are many mysteries, My Lady. Some beings have short lifespans, others live long. It is said that the Old One has existed since the beginning of time as we know it."

"Is he—" AMitY hesitated, not knowing how to phrase the question. "Is he like you—or me?"

"Who knows? No A'alude now alive has ever seen him—and the old legends become confused after so much time. But we still live by the edicts he set down for us, and we heed his warning about the Troggo. If our enemy ever finds his way into E'erwere, the bravest among us must go to warn the Old One. The trip to the citadel of the Old One, who watches over all, is long and perilous, over the mountains and across the barren desert beyond, through the land of the Golden Barbs, the swamps of the Mud People, and the valley where those strange beings who are like Gods live.

"But when our enemy comes, it must be done, My Lady, because the Troggo, with his greed for land, for gold, for slaves, would devastate not only our valley but all of E'ewere. Which is why we watch the Portal, even though it has been a hundred times a hundred suncycles since we came here to the valley."

"And in all these centuries, only two from my world have come through the Portal?" AMitY asked.

"Our legends speak of only one other—although many of the old legends have been lost. Other strangers, such as the Gra'ack and Our Lady Sab'bri, have come from different places. It is known that the Portal opens into many worlds, but for what purpose, and if all at once or one at a time we do not know. This is one of the mysteries, just as it is a mystery why only a few are summoned by the Portal."

"And yet, your ancestor brought his people through," AMitY said, her heart beating very fast as a daring thought came to her.

"This is true. The Portal permits this privilege to the favored ones."

AMitY digested this information in silence. "But why has it chosen *me?*" she mused aloud. "I'm not a prince—or anyone of importance. Why not someone like my grandfather who could be useful to you?"

"It's not our place to question the wisdom of the Portal," Lord Som'mos said, his tone rebuking. "You were the one—and none have been as welcome as you unless it was Our Lady Sab'bri and Our Lord Sojourner, who was your kind."

"His name was Sojourner?"

"So he said. This name is known to you?"

"Sojourner means—well, a traveler, one who stays for a little while."

"Ah . . . that is interesting. Yes, very interesting."

He bustled off, no doubt, AMitY thought, smiling to herself, to add this tidbit of information to his lore of legends. She sobered quickly as more questions occurred to her. The man who'd called himself Sojourner and who had been wounded in one of Earth's wars—who had he been? A soldier who kept his adventure secret for fear of being thought a liar—or insane? Or had he disguised his story as fiction?

The language he'd taught the A'aludes had a crisp,

archaic sound, very much like the formal language effected by some of the more bookish academics and ed-visors of her own time. She had once heard that, before Chaos, all citizens spoke like this. Could the Sojourner possibly have come from those decadent times? If so, Hedonist or not, he had appreciated the gentleness and simple ways of the A'aludes enough not to take advantage of them. . . .

Of all the A'aludes, though they were invariably kind and patient with her, she felt closest to Dl'lark. Perhaps because he reminded her of her own brother, or maybe just because he was more interested in her world than the others, who showed little curiosity about the way her people lived.

Of course, Dl'lark—and Wocho, his friend—did have a disconcerting habit of laughing whenever she tried to explain the Code to them, or when she recited those Litanies that warned against too-close intimacy. No amount of explaining seemed to convince them that the Litanies were not nonsense verse, like the ones A'alude children learned in the nursery.

But when she described the technology, the computers and holovision, the Sub-Trans system, the various communication and energy-producing devices, Dl'lark's eyes glowed with wonder. He was also very curious about HUmble and loved to hear about her brother's misadventures with ed-visors and disastrous chemistry experiments.

Not so oddly, it was when she was with Dl'lark and Wocho that she sometimes found her longing for her brother and grandfather almost impossible to bear. Every time she learned something new, she thought of her relatives, wishing she could share this adventure with them. How HUmble would enjoy the people, the freedom, the food here—and her grandfather could be so helpful to the A'aludes. He had been right about the Portal being a gateway into another world. Maybe *he* could explain the paradoxes of E'ewere and her own confused feelings. And maybe he could tell her why she felt so depressed at times, even though every minute was filled with something new. Was it because she missed him, and missed HUmble and PRudenCe, so much—or was it guilt because she, who didn't deserve it, was here, eating natural food, breathing air untainted by human pollution, drinking water so pure that it sparkled in the sunlight, while those who were far more deserving were back on Earth, coping with all its unsolvable problems?

"You are sad again, My Lady AMitY," Queen Aur'ri said. She had been showing AMitY how she kneaded the round loaves of bread that were a staple of the A'alude diet, then put them in tightly woven reed baskets to rise. "Come sit with me while we have teatreat, and we will talk. Perhaps it would ease your spirit if you could tell me what troubles you."

Not for the first time, AMitY was struck by the small creature's empathy. Although she knew she had no right to burden Queen Aur'ri with her problems, a few minutes later, she found herself pouring out a grief that she hadn't until this moment been able to acknowledge. As she described the Termine wards where she'd last seen her grandfather, confided her fears for HUmble, whose impatience with rules was so dangerous in a society where nonconformists were banished to the Idles or the Seafarms, Queen Aur'ri's delicate face grew grave.

And when AMitY explained what would happen to her friend PRudenCe when she reached sixteen, Queen Aur'ri's topaz-colored eyes filled with tears.

"I will make a song for them. At our next gathering, we will honor your loved ones," she said when AMitY was finished.

But she didn't say the words that AMitY desperately wanted to hear: *Your family and your friend are welcome to make their homes in the valley of the A'aludes—and so are you, My Lady AMitY.*

XIII

he next day, AMitY set about working herself into the fabric of A'aludian life.

By now, she was familiar with the daily flow of village life. She knew that in the mornings, vegetables and herbs from the gardens and fruit that had ripened in the orchards, as well as the latest crop of the peppery-tasting water herb, alissa, were gathered and brought to the cooling caves for storage. There they were apportioned out to each family in accordance with its need.

Also in the mornings, each household carried its own water from the community pump house, then took turns supplying water to the families of the baker, the slippermaker, the woodworker and other craftsmen and shopkeepers. In return, although no tokes—or any other monetary system—were used, each household received an equitable amount of bread and pastries from the baker and dairy products from the two families that processed the milk provided by the herdsmaster. The products of the skilled craftsmen were allotted according to need—with special items provided for occasions such as birthdays and anniversaries.

In addition to the specialized skill that each A'alude was responsible for, all shared in the less-favored chores of working in the mines, digging in the peat bogs, and clearing away the moss, which otherwise would have choked the fields. Even the smallest child had some daily task assigned him, if no more than to stand by in the kitchen to fetch and carry for his busy mother.

Since it was a society based on the exchange of service, AMitY looked around for a task at which she could be useful. When she came to the humbling conclusion that physical strength was her only asset, she rose early, tidied the guest cottage, then went to the stone structure built over the spring that supplied the village water.

At first, there was consternation when she filled two woven water baskets from the spring and then took up one of the carrying yokes. When she went on with her self-appointed chore of helping to fill the water troughs in the milk beasts' pen, pretending not to notice the protests, the twittering gradually stopped and, eventually, her help was accepted.

That afternoon, she helped gather the tasty water herb, alissa, from the shallow edges of the brook, then accompanied Dl'lark and Wocho, whose turn it was to search for wild herbs and nuts and berries. The next day she spend in the boggy peat fields, carrying baskets of the fuel to the community storage bins.

After she'd done her self-allotted chores for the day, she felt the need to be alone. She went off by herself, climbing up the sloping sides of the valley to sit in a patch of shade beneath a solitary tree that had taken root among the rocks.

It seemed odd to her that the A'aludes seldom did

anything alone. When one flew to the high plateau at the edge of the wilderness they called Wild Wood to pick berries or gather nuts or herbs, others went along, singing snatches of song, making a holiday of what could have been a tiresome chore. They worked side by side in the fields, in the orchards, in their kitchens; and during the long evenings when the four moons of E'ewere cast silver-and-mauve shadows over the valley, more often than not the people gathered on the village round, dressed in their finest clothes, for one of their celebrations.

It was her sixth day in E'ewere when Dl'lark and Wocho came to her quarters early to inform her that it was their turn to attend Our Lady Sab'bri.

"Today, she awakens from her rest cycle. After we see to her comfort, we'll bring back the thread she spins for us," Dl'lark told her importantly.

"May I go, too?" AMitY was very curious about this fellow traveler, who also had been chosen by the Portal, and who repaid the A'aludes' kindness with her skill as a spinner of silk.

Dl'lark's eyes glistened. "Oh, that will be termy! Her cave is near First Falls. You can climb there easily."

AMitY hid a smile. Dl'lark, who listened so avidly to her stories about HUmble, had picked up some of her brother's favorite expressions, scattering them through his conversations with blithe disregard for their correct usage.

"Are you sure your guest won't mind if I come along?"

"Our Lady Sab'bri loves company. She doesn't speak our language, but it comforts her when we sing and talk to her."

"What does she look like?" AMitY asked curiously.

"She is very pleasing to the eye, My Lady—like you. Her eyes are large, and her hair is very soft, the color of a gellums's wing."

His words evoked an image of a slender, dark-eyed woman, sitting at an ancient thread-spinning wheel such as AMitY had once seen at the N'York State Museum. *A very greedy woman* she amended an hour later when she noted the quantity of fruit and berries the children carried in their baskets.

It was a merry bunch who set out toward the cave where Our Lady Sab'bri made her home. Besides Dl'lark, Wocho and AMitY, there were three others—a tall, slender youth and two girls, one so tiny that she barely came to AMitY's knee.

In deference to AMitY, the others didn't take to the air, but frolicked around her, their high, clear voices ringing in the moist morning air. Since the baskets and wooden spindles they carried were light, AMitY insisted on carrying several of them. She would have carried more, but she was afraid of causing Offense. She also felt a little guilty, as she always did on her excursions with the children, knowing it was a hardship for them to walk instead of using their wings.

Feeling depressed suddenly, she lagged behind the others on the long climb up the rock-strewn hill. The mouth of the cave was already in sight when she heard a humming, crooning sound. The children laughed, even the serious-faced youth. They forgot their manners long enough to unfurl their wings and rise into the air.

"Our Lady Sab'bri is waiting for her food," the smallest of the girls told AMitY. She swooped down upon AMitY in a flurry of orchid-and-gold wings, seized her hand and pulled her forward. A few minutes later, they were standing just inside the narrow mouth of the cave.

After the warmth and brightness of the sunny slope, the cave seemed cool and very dark. Because of its high location, it was dry, without the dankness AMitY had expected, but there was a rich, earthy odor that made her nostrils flare.

"Put the baskets down over there," Dl'lark said. "Our Lady Sab'bri comes for her food."

AMitY dropped the baskets and spindles on one of the rush mats that covered the floor before she turned to look toward the arch of stones that led deeper into the cave. Her whole body froze as something monstrously large and black loomed there. She just had time to take in the creature's steel-blue mandibles and huge, multi-faceted eyes, its yawning mouth before she snatched up the nearest child and began to run.

The trilling voices of the children became alarmed cries, and the girl in her arms struggled to get free.

"Wait, My Lady AMitY!" Dl'lark's voice was surprisingly sharp. "Our Lady Sab'bri is our guest. She will not harm you."

It took a moment for AMitY to come to terms with her instincts, to adjust to the idea that this creature was friendly. Even so, after she let the child in her arms slip to the floor, she couldn't seem to stop shaking.

"I'm sorry. I 'spected a—" She stopped because the children, their alarm forgotten, were laughing, pushing her toward Our Lady Sab'bri.

The huge alien glided nearer, moving so easily on its hinged legs that AMitY suspected the gravity of its own world was stronger than E'ewere's. She saw that while it resembled a spider, it was something quite different. For one thing, it had four legs instead of eight. For another, its body was covered by thick, glossy hair. In its own way, it—no, *she*—was indeed beautiful.

The smallest of the girls climbed up on one of the creature's legs and began busily cleaning the razor-sharp edges of her mandibles with a pointed stick. When the others brought out brushes made of dried reed and began grooming her hair, the brilliance of Sab'bri's huge eyes dimmed, and a great rumbling sound emerged from her throat.

"Why, she's purring," AMitY said, and suddenly she was laughing with the children, mostly at her own instinctive fear of something different from herself.

When the children had brushed Sab'bri's hair until it lay sleek and smooth over her bulbous body, they fed her the fruit and berries they'd brought, chatting away as if the creature could understand, singing to her in their high, sweet voices.

"She came through the Portal, as you did," Dl'lark said, in answer to AMitY's question. "At first she was afraid and hid far back in the cave, but when she saw we meant her no harm, she came into the front chamber to eat the fruit we brought her. In gratitude, she spins her thread for us." He pointed to Sab'bri. "Look—she spins now."

A thin thread of milky fluid appeared from a small opening beneath the alien's mandibles. When it hit the air, it solidified instantly into a gleaming strand of silk, and the children began winding it onto the wooden spindles they'd brought, going about their task in such a businesslike way AMitY knew they had done it many times before.

When the spinning finally stopped and the spindles were full, Sab'bri gave a rumbling sound, almost as if she were dismissing them, and began moving backward, retreating into the cavern's inner chambers.

"How long has she been here?" AMitY asked.

"For almost three of our life-cycles. Before she came, even our gathering clothes were woven from the wool of our animals." He shook his head, looking doleful. "We are grateful for the silk, but we grieve for Our Lady Sab'bri. She is alone, cut off from her kind here. She fears the light and refuses to leave the cave. One day we hope to persuade her to return to her own world, but for now she even avoids the slanting rays of the sun that fall into the outer chamber late in the day. She is afraid of our moons, too, and goes only a few feet beyond the mouth of the cave at night—and then only when it is necessary for bodily functions."

"But if she did return to her own world, then there'd be no more silk," AMitY pointed out.

"What does that matter compared to the happiness of Our Lady Sab'bri?" Dl'lark said, looking surprised.

Before they left, the children tidied up the chamber, shaking the mats outside and filling a wooden trough with water from a nearby spring. As they gathered up the empty baskets and spindles of silk thread, AMitY couldn't help wondering how her own people would regard the largess of the silk if the creature, Sab'bri, had fallen into their hands.

It was no wonder that these gentle people had been forbidden by their protector to leave the valley, she thought soberly. The Old One had been wise enough to realize that they had no defense against predators. Even so, the Gra'ack had found them—and the Golden Barb would still be preying upon them if the Great Storm hadn't closed the pass.

Dl'lark called to her that they were ready to leave. It was evident that one of their mental exchanges had been going on because AMitY found herself relieved of the spindles she'd been carrying. The older boy and the two girls, it seemed, had volunteered to return to the village with the silk so that Dl'lark and Wocho could show AMitY yet another place where sweet herbs grew.

On a high, green meadow near the cave, they gathered the herbs, a pungent one that grew among the rocks and was used to season the bland root vegetables the A'aludes cultivated in their gardens. The boys showed AMitY how to crop only the mature outer leaves so as not to destroy the plant. After their baskets were full, they rested in the shadow of one of the valley's jumbled outcroppings of rock near a patch of dream flowers, the sweet-smelling blue flowers that grew in the high plateaus where the soil was too thin and dry for the valley's moss to thrive.

Dl'lark pointed out several nearby caves, each of which had its own name and history. At her urging, he told her more about Our Lady Sab'bri. She had passed through the Portal at night, her anguished cries as she'd fled frantically through the valley arousing the A'aludes from their sleep. Just before dawn, she had taken refuge in the cave near First Falls. No amount of persuasion since had budged her, Dl'lark added sadly.

AMitY, trying to envision the shadowy world of Sab'bri's origin, asked more questions, but Dl'lark could tell her little. Not only was Sab'bri's language incomprehensible to the A'aludes, but her mind images were too alien for them to interpret.

Dl'lark and Wocho asked AMitY to recite some of

the Litanies, which, as always, they found hilarious, then listened with flattering attention as she told them more about her own world. They never seemed to tire of hearing about the snow and harsh winters of N'York, about the triple time shifts that made it possible for so many people to live in such close quarters.

As AMitY described the Termine wards, then told them more about HUmble's school in the Artisan Swarms, she found herself suffering from unexpected pangs of homesickness. Which was all very strange, since she'd never felt at all at home in her own world, not as she did here on E'ewere.

To return to the tyranny of Cit'zen frugaLity was something she dreaded more and more. In fact, it was doubtful if she'd be allowed to stay at Grissom House now. When she'd disappeared so abruptly, what had ConCord thought? That she'd lost herself among the unDisciplined Idles? Or that she'd stolen into the O'Zones again?

And when she returned, as she must someday, how could she possibly explain her absence? If she told the truth, no one would believe her. And if she volunteered to go before the Truth machines and her story was confirmed, they would simply reason that since she believed her strange story, then she must be insane—and she would spent the rest of her life working in the plankton fields of the Sea Swarms.

She was aroused from her musings by a harsh, raucous sound. It came again, setting up a discordant echo between the cliffs. A moment later, a huge shadow swept down from above, blocking out the light. There was a pulsating noise, like a train roaring through the Sub-Trans tunnels of her own world, and then a bird-like creature with a horned head was swooping down upon them.

"The Gra'ack!" Wocho shouted as the creature landed nearby with a thump that shook the ground. Before they had time to flee, the Gra'ack swept Dl'lark up in its cruel beak and was lifting off again.

Instinct governed AMitY now. Without stopping to think, she scooped up a piece of rock the size of her hand and hurled it at the Gra'ack's hideous eyes.

There was a shriek of pain, of rage, and the Gra'ack's hold on Dl'lark loosened. Wocho, his face transformed with horror, darted forward to help AMitY as she snatched at Dl'lark's arms, jerking with all her strength. Luckily, the Gra'ack's hold was still lax; with a ripping sound, Dl'lark's tunic came loose, freeing him.

Carrying Dl'lark's limp body in her arms, AMitY raced toward a narrow opening between two jutting rocks, some part of her aware that Wocho had taken to the air and was following her. Behind them, a rush of wind that made her ears ring told her that the Gra'ack had risen, too, but she didn't look back, not even when its piercing cry came again. She concentrated every ounce of energy she possessed on speed; a few moments later, she half-fell, half-jumped into the opening between the rocks, and Wocho landed just behind her.

The cave was shallow, not much more than a depression between the jutting slabs of rock. Before she could examine Dl'lark, who was stirring in her arms, the Gra'ack's body struck the mouth of the cave, the force of the blow sending a shower of rock dust down upon their heads.

Through the narrow opening, she caught a glimpse

of the Gra'ack as it wheeled away for another assault upon the rock, and when she saw that a thick, viscous fluid covered one of its eyes, she knew where her stone had found its mark.

The next few minutes, while the creature hurled itself at the rock again and again, seemed to last forever. The three of them huddled together as far back in the depression as they could squeeze. AMitY sheltered the boys with her body as best she could, trying to keep them from seeing the sharp beak, the leathery claws that tore at the opening between the rocks just a few feet away.

"The others come," Wocho said suddenly. "They will drive the Gra'ack away now."

"But your people have no weapons," AMitY said, and because of her fear, her voice sounded accusing.

"Weapons? What is that?"

"Things to protect one's self with. Knives or swords or pointed stones—"

"Why would we need such things?" Dl'lark's voice was bewildered. "We will send the Gra'ack away with—" He hesitated, then tapped his forehead. "Of course, many must link together before the Gra'ack will heed our mind-twitch and go away." He gave her an apologetic smile. "Wocho and I forgot to watch for the Gra'ack, or he never would have gotten so close. The dream flowers made us sleepy—and then it was too late for help to reach us in time. If you hadn't hurled that rock at the Gra'ack—"

He broke off, swallowing hard. With his face sprinkled with rock dust, he looked so pitiful that AMitY's arm tightened around his small body. As both boys crept closer, she felt conflicting emotions. The

A'aludes were not as helpless as she'd believed—at least, not against a single foe. So why did she still feel such fear for them?

The Gra'ack's penetrating cry came again, reminding her that their position was still perilous. She braced herself for another of its assaults against the rock, but instead, there was a whirring sound as the giant bird rose into the air. With one final shriek, it took off, rising high above the cliffs. A few moments later, when a cloud of purple wings descended upon the plateau, AMitY closed her eyes and silently said the Litany of Thanksgiving because the ordeal was over, because the three of them had escaped serious injury—or worse.

After King L'lando, his handsome face almost as pale as his son's, had assured himself that Dl'lark was only a little bruised and shaken up, he dropped on one knee in front of AMitY, took her dust-covered hand and pressed it against his own forehead.

"My life-mate and I owe you a great debt, My Lady. The lives of our son and his cribmate are very dear to us. Ask for anything within my power to give, and it is yours."

AMitY felt an acute embarrassment at the extravagance of his offer, especially since she knew in her heart that it was undeserved. What she had done had been an instinctive act. It was only by accident that the rock she'd thrown had struck the Gra'ack in a vulnerable place. Wocho, who had come to Dl'lark's rescue without a moment's hesitation, despite his fear—and far greater danger from the Gra'ack—had been much braver than she because, of course, for all the Gra'ack's fearsomeness, it was doubtful that it could have carried away her much heavier body.

She started to point out that Wocho was the real hero—but then, as a self-serving idea came to her, she was silent. She didn't want any of the A'aludes' possessions, their gold ornaments or silk, but there was one thing, a favor, that only King L'lando could grant.

"There *is* something, King L'lando," she said, and because her need transcended shame, her voice was firm and strong.

"It is yours, My Lady AMitY," he said.

She started to speak; the words were already formed in her mind when she made the mistake of looking at Queen Aur'ri, who was holding Dl'lark in her arms. The queen's luminous eyes were steady upon hers, and in their depths AMitY read a deep sadness.

But she hardened her heart and looked away. "The thing I want is a very great favor," she said carefully.

"I have promised. It is yours," King L'lando said, but already his voice was a little stiff.

Again AMitY hesitated, but just for a moment. "I would like permission to bring my grandfather, my brother and my friend PRudenCe into the valley to live," she said.

here had been showers during the night. A mist, pearly gray in the early morning light, covered the valley floor as AMitY started up the knoll toward the Portal. Leaving behind the soft tunic and trousers, the gold-trimmed gathering gown and the slippers the A'aludes have given her, she had changed into the clothes she'd worn the day she came to E'ewere. Her coarse robe made her skin itch, her ill-fitting sandals rubbed her feet, and her belt pouch bounced uncomfortably against her hip as she climbed.

Up ahead, she saw the cairn, a gray mound in the uncertain light, and her heart beat quickened. The prospect of being back among her own kind filled her with apprehension but she felt something else, too—an anticipation, an eagerness to see other human faces. Well, in a little while she would have her wish. And, with luck, she would be returning to E'ewere with the three human beings who mattered most to her.

With luck . . . yes, she would need luck if she hoped to pull this off. She still wasn't sure what to do once she was back at Grissom House. When she'd tricked King L'lando into giving his permission for her family and

PRudenCe to make E'ewere their home, she hadn't considered the almost insurmountable odds against getting together three people who lived in separate swarms in different sections of the quad. Even if she managed that part, how could she possibly smuggle them into Grissom House, especially since she herself would probably be put into Detention as soon as she appeared?

Of course, there *was* one person who could help her—but why would ConCord, who was so out of Harmony with her, even listen? Even if she could reach him without being caught, he would surely turn her over to the Courtesy Guard immediately. Not only had she given him Insult many times, but if she told him the truth, he would think she was insane.

And it would be too dangerous, showing him the evidence she'd brought along to prove she spoke Truth—dangerous not only to herself, but to the A'aludes. So if she wanted ConCord's help, she would have to get it through trickery—which shouldn't be all that difficult for someone who had just discovered how easy it was to trick others into getting her own way.

AMitY winced, remembering how she'd taken advantage of King L'lando's gratitude and love for his son. No matter what the end result or the urgency of her motive, she wasn't proud of that—or that she could so easily consider lying to ConCord who, however angry at her now, had once cared enough about her to save her from a Life Assignment in the Subterranean Swarms.

Unconsciously, her hand dropped to the belt pouch at her waist. This morning, when she was packing the pouch for her trip, she had found her original Life Assignment slip there. Even now, the words on the

flimsy bit of paper seemed to be burned into her brain:
*Report to Apprendice Swarm 18, Ménage 43, Subterra-
nean Swarm 4, Quadrant 1. . . .*

AMitY gave her head an angry shake. The knowledge that ConCord had arranged for her to be assigned
domestic duty at Grissom House in order to save her
from the Sub-Trans Swarms had come too late. She
couldn't afford to be swayed by the realization that
she'd made a mistake, that it had been her own head-
strong nature, not ConCord, that had been her worst
enemy all along. The future of too many people was at
stake to let anything interfere with the one chance she
had to rescue her grandfather from the Termine wards,
to save PRudenCe from the cruel knives of the Medics,
to keep HUmble from ending up in the Idles—or
worse.

Near the rounded top of the knoll, she paused to
look back. From this vantage point, the cottages and
shops of the village, even the meadow where the
A'aludes gathered, were hidden from view. She had
stolen away from the guest house early to avoid good-
byes because she didn't want the A'aludes, who were so
intuitive, to sense her ambiguous feelings. Now she
wished she had asked for company. Of course, there was
the guard, whoever had been assigned watch duty at
the Portal for the night, but at this early hour, he was
probably huddled inside a warm coverlet somewhere,
dozing.

So her memories of the gathering last night would
have to sustain her until her return—or perhaps for the
rest of her life. Because there was always the possibility
that she would be trapped on Earth, unable to return.

Her feet dragging, AMitY continued her climb.
When she was standing in front of the Portal, she stared

into the churning mist. Her skin prickled with dread as another fear came to her.

She had assumed the way back was still open to her, but what if she were wrong? She knew now that the Portal opened into many other worlds. When she stepped through, would she find herself back on Earth—or in the shadowy place from which Our Lady Sab'bri had come? Or, even more chilling, in the unimaginably alien one that had spawned the Gra'ack? What if she stepped into a world whose sun had novaed—or one of such intense cold that the cells of her body would turn to ice crystals in an instant?

On the other hand, the A'aludes had been urging Our Lady Sab'bri to return to her homeworld. They seemed totally unconcerned that she might blunder into a hostile world. Was it because, having no concept of technology, they had a mystical—and erroneous—view of the Portal? Or did they know more about its mechanics than they'd told her? So often they assumed she knew what they knew, forgetting that their minds were closed to her. Often, in answer to her questions, Lord Som'mos had merely repeated vaguely that there were many mysteries, that they found it best not to question the wisdom of the Old One. . . .

"You go now, My Lady AMitY?" a voice said at her elbow.

Deep in her own thoughts, AMitY hadn't seen Dl'lark's approach. She smiled as she took in the woebegone expression on his small face.

"It's just for a little while, Prince Dl'lark. I'll be back soon with my fam'ly and friend." In an effort to elicit a smile, she added, "My brother will have many 'ventures with you and Lord Wocho, I s'pect."

But Dl'lark's face didn't brighten. "You are afraid

that your people won't let you return to E'ewere," he said accusingly.

"How do you know this?"

Dl'lark winced at the sharpness in her voice. "What one of us knows, all knows," he said with dignity. "You told my mother about your fears last night at the gathering."

AMitY relaxed, a little ashamed of her quick suspicion. As she remembered that bittersweet celebration now, she sighed deeply. Never had the air-dancers seemed more graceful or the singing more haunting. In her sorrow at having to leave it all behind, even briefly, she'd forgotten her determination to remain cheerful— at least, outwardly—on this last night and had confided some of her secret fears to Queen Aur'ri. And now Dl'lark was troubled by those fears.

"It will all work out," she said, forcing a smile. "I'll ask an old friend for help—and when I return with the others, maybe your people will have a gather'n for us. Right now, I'm 'cerned 'bout someth'n else. Lord Som'mos tells me the Portal opens into many worlds besides my own. How do I know that when I step through, I won't find myself on an alien planet, one dangerous to my kind?"

Dl'lark gave her a wondering look. "But you must not think such thoughts, My Lady AMitY! Fill your mind with images of your Earth and all will be well."

AMitY hid her doubts and nodded. "Then this is goodbye—but just for a little while."

She hesitated, then bent to kiss his small face. Despite her gradual acceptance of the ways of the A'aludes, who kissed on all occasions, she knew her cheeks were flushed as she turned away quickly to face the Portal. Holding an image of the attic room in her mind, she took one last breath of E'ewere's sweet-scented air and then slid quickly through the Portal, afraid that if she hesitated even one second longer, she would never again find the courage to leave.

There was a flicker of nausea, so fleeting that she wasn't sure she hadn't imagined it, followed by a cold so intense that it curdled her flesh. She caught a glimpse of an alien landscape, gray as cinders, breathed in an air so sulphuric that it burned her throat. In terror, she closed her eyes tightly, concentrated on an image of her grandfather's face, and when she was forced to breathe again, the air she inhaled was dank and stale and reeking of mildew.

She opened her eyes and found herself standing in the small niche under the eaves of Grissom House. When she turned to look through the window behind her, she saw a patch of gray winter sky and the top of a neighboring Museum House.

The ceiling above her head seemed to be moving down upon her, and she realized she was in a stage of near panic. Just as she'd been afraid that she might be trapped on an alien world, unable to return to Earth or E'ewere, now her fear was that she'd exiled herself forever on Earth. Knowing she must do something to break the spiraling fear, she pressed her fingertips against her forehead and summoned up a Litany.

I am a vessel.
Let me be filled with Peace,
So that I may think with clarity and humility;
And never forget that I am but one of many,
A small part of the whole.
I am a vessel.
Let me be filled with Peace.

The familiar words soothed her; the fear began to abate. By the time the Litany had spun through her mind, the attack of claustrophobia was gone, but she stood there a few minutes longer, breathing deeply, listening to the distant sound of traffic and the winter wind whining at the corners of the roof.

Cautiously, she approached the trapdoor, a dim square in the splintery floorboards. When she pulled at the piece of wood, rusty hinges squealed a protest, and she paused, her mouth dry. It was a few seconds before she found the courage to lift it far enough so she could peer through the opening.

In the sleep alcove below, a single safety light cast a green glow over empty bunks and folded sleep cocoons. There was no way of telling if it were late morning or early evening, but for the present, her cove-mates were gone.

Even so, AMitY felt a reluctance to leave the safety of the attic. The variables were so many that it was pointless to plan beyond this point. She would try to reach ConCord, and if that failed and she were caught, then she would demand to be taken to him. It was all a matter of luck now.

Moving quietly, she eased her legs through the trapdoor opening until she was kneeling on her bunk. Her sleep cocoon, which should have been folded neatly at the end of the bunk, was gone, bringing home her plight should she be discovered before she reached ConCord's chambers.

Reaching up, she let down the trapdoor. Although she knew she couldn't afford to waste any time, she lingered a few seconds staring up at the small square above her before she climbed down from the bunk and tiptoed across the narrow room. When she opened the door a cautious half-inch, she discovered that the hall outside was empty. From the canteen a few doors away, she heard the murmuring of voices and knew the other domestics were eating either first- or thirdmeal.

ConCord's chambers were located on the floor below the domestic quarters. With luck, she could reach them without being seen. And if ConCord wasn't there? Well, then she would hide somewhere until he appeared. . . .

But her luck ran out as she was hurrying down the service stairs. She had almost reached the floor below when the door she was approaching opened and Citizen frugaLity came through.

Under different circumstances, AMitY might have enjoyed the shock on the chief domestic's usually impassive face. In her surprise, the woman's breath escaped in a long, sibilant hiss. But the fury that replaced the surprise was so menacing that AMitY instinctively backed away, her leg muscles tensed for flight.

"So you 'cided to r'turn, Cit'zen AMitY. I s'pose you've 'cocted some wild story to 'splain your absence?"

After the A'aludes' crisp pronunciations, the woman's slurred words seemed slovenly, difficult to understand, and it was a moment before AMitY responded.

"I don't un'stand, Cit'zen frugaLity," she said, trying to sound bewildered. "I had p'mission to take"—she paused, realizing she wasn't sure how long, in Earth time, she'd been gone—"a few Free-days off from my duties."

"What's this, cit'zen? Have you added unTruth to your other crimes?"

"But I speak Truth, Cit'zen frugaLity. I s'gest you

take me to Cit'zen ConCord so we can clear this th'n up."

"I've no 'tention of bother'n Cit'zen ConCord with such a triv'al matter, 'specially since he's been gone for the past six days and just r'turned this morn'n. But when I 'formed him of your unauth'rized absence just 'fore he left, he said noth'n to me 'bout any Free-days."

"Maybe he had more 'portant th'n's on his mind. I 'spect'ly 'quest you talk to him 'fore you do anyth'n that could be—'barrass'n."

Citizen frugaLity's lips tightened, but there was a flicker of uncertainty in her eyes now. Maybe she remembered that ConCord had gotten AMitY her assignment at Grissom House because she shrugged finally.

"You can be sure we'll get to the bottom of this. If you've been telling unTruths, you'll have *two* charges to answer to, young cit'zen."

She turned on her heel and stalked off down the hall; even the rustle of her robe had an ominous sound. As AMitY followed her, she found it hard to remember how impressed with the wonders of Grissom House she'd once been. Now, having experienced the simple comfort of the A'aludes' cottages, the artistry of their wall hangings and gold ornaments, the hall, with its walls cluttered with faded posters and graphics, its worn, plastic-protected floor and its collection of antique metal chairs, had a dreary, sad look.

Citizen frugaLity stopped in front of the room where AMitY had once encountered ConCord. At her rap, ConCord opened the door. He seemed subtly to have aged since the last time AMitY had seen him, perhaps because of the dark shadows under his eyes and the gauntness of his face.

"What is it, Cit'zen frugaLity? I left orders I wasn't to be—" He broke off as his eyes moved past the chief domestic's angular figure. For a moment, until a mask dropped over his face, the relief there was so naked that AMitY relaxed slightly, knowing that however angry with her he might be, ConCord still cared enough to be glad that she was safe.

She forced the corners of her stiff lips upward, and because it was so important to enlist his sympathy, she consciously imitated the warm smiles of the A'aludes. Although ConCord didn't smile back, he stared at her so intently that, a couple of weeks earlier, she would have flushed and looked away in confusion.

"So you've 'turned, Cit'zen AMitY," he said, his voice without inflection.

AMitY bowed deeply, letting her cowl slip down to hide her eyes. "Yes, Cit'zen ConCord-Grissom," she murmured. "I know you gave me p'mission to take several 'ditional Free-days, but I 'cided to come back early."

When he was silent, she risked a quick glance at him from the shelter of her cowl and found him watching her, a bemused look on his face.

"You 'cided to come back early, did you? Now why would you do that?" he asked, as if curious to see what she would come up with next.

"I didn't want to take 'vantage of our—our friendship," she said.

"Ver' Harmon'ous of you." There was no mistaking the irony in his voice now. AMitY was relieved when he addressed his next question to Citizen frugaLity. "You brought Cit'zen AMitY here for some special reason?"

Citizen frugaLity's face was a study of uncertainty—and suspicion. "May I 'spect'ly ask why I wasn't told that you'd given Cit'zen AMitY p'mission to take Free-time, Cit'zen ConCord-Grissom?"

"It was an ov'sight. I'm 'fraid I had so much on my mind that I forgot. And since I've been gone the past few days on other bus'ness, I didn't think of it 'gain. I 'sure you this is the last time anyth'n like this will happen."

This time, he looked directly into AMitY's eyes, and the grimness in his voice told her that while she was past the first hurdle, she still hadn't succeeded in disarming him completely.

"Well, it's all ver' unOrth'dox. I 'ported Cit'zen AMitY miss'n to the Code Guard. There's sure to be questions—"

"I'll take care of all that. And now, if you'll 'scuse us, I have some private bus'ness with Cit'zen AMitY."

Although Citizen frugaLity bowed silently, her eyes glittered as if she had a high fever as she turned and left the room.

AMitY didn't give ConCord time to speak first. "I 'pol'gize for the unTruth," she said quickly. "I went 'way 'cause I needed time 'lone to—"

"Where in Harmony have you been?" ConCord interrupted roughly.

"In—in the Idles."

The frown on ConCord's face deepened. "I can un'stand why you feel you have to lie to Cit'zen frugaL-ity, but why are you ly'n to me?"

When AMitY gasped, his eyes narrowed with scorn. "Does the word *lie* Offend you, Cit'zen? It's meaning fits the occasion, and I notice that the *act* doesn't bother you at all, since you've done quite a lot of it in the past few minutes. Now I ask you again—where have you been hid'n out?"

"I told you. In the Idles."

"Don't c'pound your sins with more lies." He reached out and jerked her cowl back from her face. "And don't try to hid 'hind your priv'cy cowl either. You've been in the O'Zones. Look at the color of your skin. Where else would you get such a tan?"

AMitY stared down at her telltale hands. Why hadn't she realized that her tanned skin would give her away? And of course ConCord *would* believe that she'd been hiding out in the O'Zones. He, of all people, knew that she wasn't afraid of its dangers, real or imagined.

She realized ConCord was waiting for an explanation and suddenly she knew that, for now, she didn't want to tell him any more unTruths—no, any more *lies*. Because he was right. It was hypocritical to balk at using the swear word when she had so easily done the deed.

So instead of answering his question, she said, "You haven't asked me why I came back."

"Very well. Why *did* you r'turn? Did it get too cold for you in the O'Zones—or did you run out of food?"

"While I was gone, I found this." AMitY took the Life Assignment slip from her belt pouch and showed it to ConCord. "I was too out of Harmony Comp Day to read it 'fore I dropped it into my belt pouch, and then I forgot 'bout it. But now I un'stand why you 'ranged for me to be 'signed to Grissom House. I want to 'pol'gize for—for misjudg'n your motives."

She waited, her eyelids lowered. When the silence between them lengthened, when she finally couldn't stand the suspense any longer, she looked up. ConCord was smiling, an odd smile that told her he believed her—but that he, who knew how hard apologies came to her, was also enjoying her discomfiture.

How easy it is to lie, she thought bitterly—*and how vulnerable those who live by the Code are to people like me.*

She realized her face was burning, that ConCord, always so observant, was no longer smiling. She rushed into speech. "Do you f'give me, ConCord?" she asked.

ConCord ran his hand over his face. His beard, always so neatly trimmed since he'd passed his twenty-first birthday, had a neglected look as if he'd been too busy to bother with his personal appearance lately.

"Yes, I f'give you," he said heavily. "You must know by now that I'd f'give you 'most anyth'n, AMitY. Do you have an idea what I've been through since Cit'zen frugaLity told me you were miss'n? I've been comb'n the Idles, the O'Zones, the Art'san Swarms, look'n for you. I was sure you'd done someth'n rash, like go'n into the Outlands, that you were—" He broke off, his eyes haunted.

"I'm sorry," she said, and discovered that just by saying the words out loud, she really meant them—but not enough to keep her from adding, her voice whisper soft, "If I'd been caught, would you've helped me?"

ConCord's eyes turned opaque. "Why do you ask that?"

"It's 'portant to me to know if—if you're still out of Harmony with me."

"Yes, I would've helped you." A smile warmed ConCord's face. "But first I would've made you suffer a little."

"I've done so many stupid th'n's, ConCord—why do you still care what happens to me?"

" 'Cause I see someth'n special in you. A willing-ness to step beyond the bound'ries of this narrow world of ours, to take chances and seek new d'rections, to strike out into the unknown. That's why I want you at my side on the Outland expedition, AMitY."

"I want to be the girl you think I am," she said, but even to her own ears, her voice sounded hollow. If her plan worked out, she wouldn't be here to go beyond the Barriers with ConCord. . . .

"Then let's forget what happened, now that we're friends again—we are friends, aren't we, AMitY?"

"Friends—and more," she said softly.

"You've changed." The pucker was back between ConCord's eyebrows. "It isn't just your 'pearance—though I do wonder how you managed to gain weight in the O'Zones. Suddenly, you seem so—so mature."

"I had time 'lone to think—and then I found that 'signment slip and realized what a fool I'd been. That's when I knew I didn't want you to be my en'my."

ConCord regarded her with steady eyes. "I've never been your en'my, AMitY. Even when you were your most ag'vat'n, I've always been your friend."

AMitY discovered a tightness inside her chest. This was what she'd hoped for—so why did she sud-denly want to cry? "Thank you for be'n so kind to HUmble," she said. "And for lending your books to my grandfather."

At ConCord's quick frown, she added, "He didn't tell me. But who else does my grandfather know who still owns books?" She paused, choosing her next words with care. "I once r'fused to go to an Old Town Torium concert with you. Now I'd like to ask 'nother favor in-stead. My grandfather and brother and my friend,

Cit'zen PRudenCe must be worried 'bout me. Would it be pos'ble for us to meet in a priv'cy booth somewhere?"

"That would be a ver' crowded priv'cy booth, I'm 'fraid. Why don't you meet here at Grissom House? Maybe your fam'ly and friend would enjoy a house tour, too. I'll take care of out-of-mènage permits and mo'cart trans'tation—would that please you, AMitY?"

Not daring to trust her voice, AMitY nodded.

"Then leave it to me. S'pose we make it three days from now? As for Cit'zen frugaLity, I'll speak to her. While you were gone, I learned a few th'n's that—well, let's say my mother has 'lowed our chief 'mestic too much freedom in run'n Grissom House. I knew noth'n 'bout her treatment of you till one of the staff came to me this morn'n and told me what's been go'n on. When you were first 'signed here, I told Cit'zen frugaLity you weren't to be given any special priv'leges. I s'pect she drew her own 'clusions from that."

"Please—it would be better if you said noth'n to Cit'zen frugaLity," AMitY said quickly.

"Ver' well. It prob'ly isn't nec'sary. I'm sure she won't take 'vantage of her position again." He paused, and now he was smiling again. "And I think you'd better r'turn to 'mestic quarters 'fore your rep'tation is ruined for good. 'Sides, it's gett'n more dif'cult ev' moment for me to observe the Disciplines with you smil'n at me like that, AMitY. I know it's too early to talk 'bout the future, so all I'll say now is that I'm glad you're back—and that I'm not go'n to let misun'stand'n's come 'tween us 'gain."

AMitY bowed formally and left the room, glad that she didn't have to face his clear gaze any longer.

How easy, how very easy it was to manipulate

others, she thought with self-loathing. Would her second disappearance turn ConCord bitter, alter the direction of his life? She hoped it wouldn't, but even if she knew for sure it would—what choice did she have? Because nothing had changed. Her grandfather was still trapped in the deadly stagnation of a Termine ward. At any minute, HUmble's rebellious nature could land him in real trouble—and even if ConCord's influence prevented that, what could he do for PRudenCe, who would be sixteen in a few days?

No, she mustn't, *couldn't* weaken. How could she take chances with the lives of three other people just when everything was going so well? So she had no choice—but that didn't mean she didn't feel ashamed of what she had done, did it?

The shame stayed with AMitY during the next three days while she returned to her duties as an Apprentice Domestic. It didn't help alleviate her guilt to discover that her status had changed dramatically since her return. At one time, she would have welcomed the friendliness of her fellow domestics. Now, knowing how short-lived it must be, she found herself wishing they would ignore her as they had in the past. How could she take any pleasure in their Courtesies when she knew that it stemmed from their certainty that she was back in favor with ConCord?

In fact, she discovered she much preferred the unrelenting hostility of Cit'zen frugaLity. Although the chief domestic no longer demanded extra hours of work from her, the balefulness in her eyes when they met was unchanged. AMitY, who had just discovered her own unexpected talent for duplicity, couldn't help feeling a grudging respect for the woman's open—and unhypocritical—dislike.

Two days later, ConCord sent for her to tell her that he had made all the arrangements for her family and PRudenCe to visit Grissom House.

"After they've taken the tour," he added, "I've 'ranged for 'freshments to be served to your guests in my private chambers. And I have a special s'prise for Cit'zen PRudenCe. I've 'ranged for her young sister and her friend, Cit'zen UNison, to be included in the party."

MitY didn't need the buzz of the alcove's sleep monitor to arouse her from her cocoon the next morning. She had been awake most of the night. Somehow she'd managed not to Offend her cove-mates by excessive tossing and turning, but she hadn't been able to control her overactive mind. During the long hours of the night, her thoughts had returned again and again to the problems she could expect the next day. A dozen new dangers had reared their heads—and she had devised a dozen new variations to her plan in case they were needed.

It *will* succeed, she thought again. Getting six people instead of four through the Portal presented added difficulties—but it must be done. And wasn't it odd that this was one thing she hadn't even considered in her original plan, that in ConCord's eagerness to please her, he might add two more guests?

Before she'd left E'ewere, she'd prepared herself for the doubts of PRudenCe and her own family, but Tutu was a total stranger to her—and UNison nearly so. What if they thought she was lying? Or insane? Would they think it their duty to report her, as the Code demanded?

When she tried to recall what she knew about PRudenCe's younger sister, she realized it was very little. PRudenCe seemed reluctant to talk about Tutu. If it were someone else, she might even think that PRudenCe was ashamed of her sister's illegal status, but she knew her friend too well. Once, when she'd asked how Tutu was getting along at the School for Illegals where she'd lived most of her eleven years, PRudenCe's answer had been so evasive that she'd politely changed the subject. Now, with so much depending upon Tutu's reaction, AMitY wished she'd questioned her friend further.

And what about Citizen UNison? He'd been pleasant enough the two times she'd met him, and yet—there'd been something, a boldness, about the way he'd looked at her that had made her uncomfortable. If PRudenCe had chosen him for a bondmate, it wasn't her place to make judgments, but even so, his quoting of the Litanies had struck her as being excessive, especially since she knew, from things PRudenCe had let drop, that UNison was bitter about his Life Assignment. Not, AMitY thought, that she could fault him for that. Was she any better? She'd resented her own assignment bitterly. As for wanting to better his status—what about ConCord and his unwavering determination to explore the Outlands? Why didn't she feel that *his* zeal was excessive?

And anyway, she had no choice but to include UNison and Tutu in her plans. Even if she could talk ConCord into arranging another meeting, time had almost run out for PRudenCe, whose sixteenth birthday was so close. Not only must she persuade all of them, including Tutu and Citizen UNison, to return with her to E'ewere, but she must convince them to go today, leaving their old lives behind. . . .

Two hours later, as AMitY waited at the main entrance of Grissom House for her party to arrive, she was aware of the oblique glances of the Courtesy Guardsman on duty. To defuse his curiosity, she kept her privacy cowl lowered and stayed in the shadows of the gloomy reception hall. It didn't help her conscience, knowing that Citizen frugaLity's disapproval of this unheard of privilege for an Apprentice Domestic would be justified in a few hours, that soon the whole quadrant would be buzzing with rumors about Grissom House.

Would the scandal adversely effect ConCord's plans for an Outlands expedition? Even though he was the son of the state's Chief Arbitrator and immune to the restrictions of ordinary citizens, he did need the goodwill of the Council of Nine—and they might not be eager to grant permission for such a risky venture to someone who was involved in the mysterious disappearance of six citizens.

The knowledge that she was repaying ConCord's kindness with betrayal plagued AMitY as she greeted her grandfather and brother a few minutes later with a low bow and the whispered assurance that all was well with her, that she would explain everything shortly.

When PRudenCe arrived, accompanied by her sister, AMitY studied the child curiously. Her first impression was that Tutu, with her dusky skin and glossy black hair, was a smaller replica of PRudenCe, but when she met Tutu's unblinking stare, she realized the resemblance was superficial. There was none of PRudenCe's warmth in those dark eyes, and Tutu's bow was more the gesture of a citizen greeting an inferior than that of a child with an adult.

Her uneasiness deepened as PRudenCe drew her aside to murmur softly, "Be careful what you say 'round Tutu. She—she might misun'stand our jokes and 'sider it her duty to 'port us to her ed-visors."

At AMitY's involuntary frown, she added quickly, "I'm sure she'll change when she's older, but she's been so 'doctr'ated at her school that she's someth'n of a Zealot."

Uneasily, AMitY looked around and found PRudenCe's sister watching her. Something cold and too-adult in those black eyes told her that any attempts to persuade Tutu to accompanying her through the Portal would fall on deaf ears. She also doubted that adulthood would change Tutu. Zealots, she had come to realize, seldom changed with age—except to grow more rigid and intolerant.

Citizen UNison arrived last, full of importance because he'd been transported from his bachelors' ménage to Old Town in a government mo'cart. He was a stocky, dark-haired man in his early twenties, with a self-assured manner at odds, AMitY privately thought, with his low status. Although he returned PRudenCe's and AMitY's bow, he was so busy staring around the reception hall that he didn't notice Citizen ausTere, who, as the oldest there, should have received his first bow.

The tour of the public viewing rooms took almost an hour. To AMitY, who had seen the workmanship of A'alude wood carvers and goldsmiths, these unlovely and sometimes battered relics of Earth's past seemed a little pitiful. But the others were so impressed by the ancient communication devices, the pieces of pottery and glass that had survived the centuries, the resin-protected photographs that dated back to the first days of Chaos that she drew some pleasure from their enjoyment. Her grandfather's eyes gleamed as he examined the titles of the books, each encased in its own transparent protector, and HUmble viewed everything from the collection of antique plastics to pre-Chaos coins with his usual curiosity.

As AMitY watched the absorbed faces of her two men, so alike despite the disparity of their ages, her faith that she was doing the right thing was reaffirmed. Even though there were two new factors, Tutu and Citizen UNison, she told herself, she must go ahead with her plan.

At the end of the tour, she dismissed the guide, saying that she would see her guests upstairs to Citizen ConCord's chambers, where refreshments were waiting for them. It was an indication of her changed status that the guide, her elder by at least six years, bowed and left without argument.

Since she half-expected ConCord to be waiting for them in his study, she was relieved to find the room empty. As she suggested that her guests be seated, something in her manner must have alerted the others because they watched her with a variety of expressions on their faces. She was sure she saw concern in her grandfather's eyes, and there was no doubting her brother's curiosity or PRudenCe's worry, but what emotions lay behind Tutu's stony stare and UNison's frown?

Avoiding PRudenCe's eyes, she gave Tutu directions to the domestics' canteen and told her to go help carry their refreshments downstairs. Tutu's lower lip protruded rebelliously; there was something too knowing about the way she looked first at her sister, then at AMitY before she lowered her gaze and silently left the room.

AMitY waited until the sound of Tutu's footsteps had retreated down the hall before she spoke. "There's a decision you must make today, but first I want to show you—these."

From her belt pouch, she took out three objects and laid them on ConCord's desk. She stood back then, watching their faces as they stared at the gold bracelet Prince Gw'wanna had given her, at a richly embroidered scarf that had been a gift from Queen Aur'ri— and at a small fruit-filled tart that she'd wrapped carefully in the scarf before she put it in her belt pouch four evenings earlier.

 t took AMitY only a few minutes to tell the bare bones of her adventures in E'ewere. It took longer to convince her listeners that she was speaking Truth, that she wasn't indulging in some escapist fantasy. But with the gold bracelet, the silk scarf, the small brown tart lying there on the desk, how could they doubt the evidence of their own eyes?

Not so surprisingly, it was HUmble who first agreed to accompany AMitY to E'ewere. "When do we leave?" he said, looking hungrily at the stale, but still succulent-looking pastry.

"Yes—we have to go," Citizen ausTere said, nodding. It seemed to AMitY that her grandfather had suddenly become infused with new life as she'd described the Portal, the A'aludes, the wonders of E'ewere. "Have you thought of a way to get us into this secret room you've found, granddaughter?"

"No one will question us," AMitY said, hoping she spoke Truth. "The staff b'lieves that—that Cit'zen ConCord has put in a First Pair'n bid for me. So I don't 'spect any dif'culties 'less we meet Cit'zen frugaLity, the chief 'mestic. Luck'ly, with the whole household on Second Time, ev'body is busy this time of day so my sleep 'cove should be empty."

Citizen UNison had been studying the gold bracelet, which seemed to fascinate him. He looked up now. "What about Cit'zen Tutu? PRudenCe tells me she's a Zealot. I think we should leave 'fore she r'turns."

"Oh, I couldn't go without Tutu!" PRudenCe protested. She had been stroking the scarf with the tips of her fingers as if afraid it would vanish any moment. "She doesn't have to know our plans 'forehand. I'm sure she'll realize later that this is for her own good."

AMitY, remembering Tutu's self-righteous comments about Decadence and Hedonism during their tour of the house, wasn't so sure, but she remained silent, knowing her friend's stubbornness. Better to be burdened with Tutu than to leave PRudenCe behind to be banished to the Sterie Swarms. . . .

They were still making plans when Tutu and one of the domestics arrived, bearing trays of food. After they'd finished the tea-treat, the soytein bars and dried apple wedges ConCord had ordered for them, AMitY was careful not to look at Tutu as she said, "I have p'mission from Cit'zen ConCord-Grissom to give you a tour of the 'mestic quarters so you can see how I live here in Old Town."

A few minutes later, as she led the others up the service stairs, she found it hard to control her anxiety. Every second, she expected to be challenged by one of the older domestics—or by Citizen frugaLity. Even if the chief domestic didn't dispute her word openly, she might well insist on accompanying them on their tour, since it was rare for visitors to invade the privacy of the domestic quarters.

So it was with relief that AMitY finally opened the door of her sleep alcove. When she was sure the room was empty, she motioned the others inside and then quickly closed the door behind them. "Climb up on the top bunk," she told HUmble. "Push open the trapdoor and then you can help Tutu up—"

A hissing sound startled her into silence. She turned to face Tutu's suspicious glare. In the green-tinged light, her thin face had a sallow, pinched look. "Why did you tell Cit'zen HUmble to help me up on the bunk? Surely, that's a Decorum Lapse!"

"Do what Cit'zen AMitY tells you," PRudenCe said quickly. "I'll 'splain later."

Tutu's response was to edge toward the door.

"I want to show you a recently discovered secret room," AMitY improvised. "It isn't open to the public yet, but—"

"Then why are show'n it to us? I've heard 'bout the loose ways of Old Town 'mestics. Don't you 'serve Decorum at Grissom House, Cit'zen AMitY?"

HUmble gave a disgusted snort. "Oh, for laugh'n out loud in public! Don't act so termy, Cit'zen Tutu. It'll be whiz, 'splor'n a secret room, someth'n to tell your mates when you get back to school."

Tutu's mouth opened, but before she could speak, Cit'zen ausTere told her, "Your dil'gence to the Code is admir'ble, young cit'zen, but in this case, it's misplaced. Now do as your sister tells you."

Tutu's face was still sullen, but she was too used to following the edicts of her ed-visors to challenge the direct order of an elder citizen. Silently, she followed

HUmble up the bunk ladder, then crouched there, looking like a small, disagreeable monkey, while he opened the trapdoor and hoisted himself through the opening.

But when HUmble reached his hand down to her, she refused his help with a hiss of Offense. Agile and quick, she slid unaided through the trapdoor. PRudenCe and UNison followed, then helped Citizen ausTere through, with AMitY bringing up the rear. By the time she was standing in the enclosure, her head ached with tension.

The space was so cramped that it was necessary for the group to stand close together. AMitY sensed their embarrassment at having their personal space invaded as they waited for her next move. For the first time, a new question occurred to her. How would these people, products of a culture that forbade touching or even laughing in public, adjust to the stroking, the cuddling and kissing that was as natural to the A'aludes as breathing? Would they learn to accept a way of life so different from their own—or would they be repulsed by the simple, childlike affection of the A'aludes?

As she turned to close the trapdoor, Tutu's disgruntled voice stopped her. "There's noth'n to see here. It's just an empty room!"

"I have a s'prise for you," AMitY said. "We're go'n to watch a ver' special holo-play."

She edged around UNison until she was facing the window. Closing her eyes for better concentration, she let her mind fill with images of E'ewere. At first, the light against her eyelids remained dim, reflecting the overcast sky outside. When it brightened, her relief was so strong that she felt giddy as she opened her eyes and stared hungrily at E'ewere.

It was early evening in the valley. Long, silvery-blue shadows grew from the trunks of the trees, from the base of the cliff and the moss-covered rock sentinels that littered the valley. Below, she saw the cheerful light of an open peatfire and knew that the A'aludes were keeping watch for her.

Mutely, she turned to the others, who had been silent, and pointed at the window. HUmble crowded up beside her.

"It's just like my dreams," he said, his voice awed.

Behind him, Citizen ausTere cleared his throat. "I'm 'fraid I only see a stained glass window."

Tutu edged closer to the open trapdoor. "I want to leave. It's dusty here—and ev'body act'n ver' un-Orth'dox," she whimpered.

"Open your eyes, Cit'zen Tutu," HUmble said impatiently. "The valley's right there—as plain as the pouch on your belt.

AMitY rubbed her temples, trying to think. Something was wrong—had she made a mistake, believing that just by willing it, she could take them through the Portal? If they couldn't see it, how could she convince the others that E'ewere really existed, to trust her enough to step through what seemed to them to be a dusty window, four stories above the street?

From the corner of her eye, she caught the suspicion on UNison's face, PRudenCe's disappointment—or was that relief she saw on her friend's face? An idea came to her. Before anyone could guess her intention, she turned toward the window and stepped over the sill, knowing it must look as if she were passing through the glass panels. There was a flash of nausea, stronger than the last time, a painful prickling of her skin, and then she was standing on the grass-moss of E'ewere, the soft evening breeze whipping her robe against her legs.

Knowing she must return immediately before the others panicked, she turned back to the Portal. Something moved inside the turbulent mist; a moment later, HUmble was standing beside her.

For a long moment, he stared at the shadow-filled valley, then up at Our Lord Luk'ko and his three sister moons. "Top-o," he said.

AMitY wanted to hug him, but she smiled at him instead. "I'll go back and get the others." She hesitated, then added. "There's always a slight chance that someth'n could go wrong. If that should happen, don't look back. Make a life for yourself here."

She didn't give him a chance to ask questions. Quickly, she turned and slid into the gray mist. This time, the nausea was worse, almost as if the Portal were warning her that those who passed through too often must pay a toll. But before she could panic, she was standing in the attic of Grissom House, watching the fear on her grandfather's face change to relief.

"Thank Harmony you're safe," he said. "When you and HUmble dis'peared, we thought—" He didn't finish the sentence. Instead, he shook his head, looking regretful. "I'm 'fraid the rest of us can't 'comp'ny you into E'ewere, granddaughter."

"But you can! The Portal p'mitted the A'aludes to pass through once one of them was 'tuned to it—"

"The A'aludes, from what you tell me, are telepathic. We humans are not. It was a won'ful dream, but it's only for you and HUmble. R'turn to E'ewere. You'll be safe there."

"But I can't leave you. If you'll just conc'trate, I'm sure you'll see—"

"I don't want to stay here," Tutu interrupted rudely. Her lower lip protruded ominously. "You're talk'n strange—and where did that boy go? He was stand'n by that window and then he was gone."

AMitY ignored her. Of all the possible obstacles that she'd considered, this one she hadn't foreseen. She'd been so sure that once they had reached the attic room, the rest would be easy.

"What's tak'n you so long?" It was HUmble; from his cheeky grin, he'd had no difficulty passing back through the Portal. "It's really ding-dong in E'ewere, just like I thought it would be." When no one spoke, he gave an impatient shrug. "Come on, Cit'zen Tutu. I'll take you through."

Before Tutu could move, he had grabbed her hand. She gave a shriek of fear as he half-dragged, half-yanked her over the sill. The glow intensified, then dimmed as both youngsters disappeared.

Realization came to AMitY in a rush of relief. "Of course—I have to *touch* you and lead you through." She caught UNison's recoil. "I'm sorry, Cit'zen UNison, but it's the only way."

"I'll go first," PRudenCe said bravely, but her face was pale as she extended her hand.

A few minutes later, they were all standing in the deepening shadows of the valley, looking dazed and, in PRudenCe's case, more than a little frightened. Citizen ausTere was the first to recover his equilibrium.

He retreated a few feet from the cairn of rocks to stare up at the moss-covered carvings about the Portal, now barely visible in the fading light. For a long time, he studied the marks before he turned his attention to the small crystal dome set into the frame. When he pushed back his cowl to get a better look, AMitY noticed that with his face so alive with interest he looked almost as young as UNison, who seemed subtly to have aged in the past few minutes.

PRudenCe, who was kneeling on a mound of moss, looked up at AMitY. Although her face was pale, she managed a smile. "It's just like you said it was. I still can't b'lieve—"

A wail interrupted her. Tutu, looking like a pile of discarded rags, was huddled at the foot of the cairn, her small body wracked with sobs.

"Poor child," Citizen ausTere said, shaking his head. "Perhaps it would've been kinder to leave her 'hind."

But AMitY had more pressing worries at the moment than Tutu's distress. It had just come to her that, in her haste to placate Tutu earlier, she had left the trapdoor open. When their disappearance became evident, Citizen frugaLity would surely order a search of the house. The open trapdoor would lead to the discovery of the attic room—and to six sets of footprints in the dust, all ending at a window that had been sealed shut for more than a century.

AMitY felt a prickle of guilt. She had seen how rumors proliferated in the Swarms, how the least hint of something out of the ordinary could sweep through the ménages and become twisted and ugly. There had been incidents—the shunning of the occupants of a so-called haunted sleeping bay where two citizens had fallen to their deaths from upper bunks; a citizen who'd become a pariah because he'd been unlucky enough to be assigned to three separate swarms that had caught fire.

She didn't want that to happen here, to have Con-Cord's family besmirched by scandal and rumor. Their disappearance would cause enough embarrassment for ConCord, who had authorized the tour for her group. She owed it to him not to let it become something more than a minor mystery.

And there was another, more personal consideration. If the attic room was discovered, it would surely become an object of curiosity. Who knew how many citizens would come here to inspect it? It was dangerous to take it for granted that the Portal was open only to HUmble and her. What if someone else had the right brainwaves and could pass through the Portal? No, she couldn't take that chance. Much as she dreaded another passage through the Portal, she must go back one more time to close the trapdoor.

During her debate with herself, the others had recovered from their initial awe—and in Tutu's case, terror. There was a babble of sound as they all seemed to find their voices at the same time.

AMitY interrupted her grandfather, who was saying something about a force field. "I have to go back to close the trapdoor," she said.

She expected an argument, but instead Citizen ausTere nodded agreement. "Yes, you must close it. I 'spect the Portal is only rarely 'tuned to a brainwave pattern, but it's always poss'ble that you and HUmble aren't unique." He paused, the worry in his eyes belying his casual tone. "Be careful—and r'turn 'med'ately, AMitY."

"I'll be careful," she promised.

As she faced the mist again, AMitY fought against a reluctance more to do with the Portal itself than with her fear of being trapped on Earth. Later, she would tell her grandfather about her suspicion that there was a limit to how many times she could safely pass between worlds. For now, it was kinder to let him believe it was merely a matter of stepping into the mist and coming out the other side.

But this time, paradoxically, there was no nausea, no painful prickling of her skin, no images of worlds so alien that they made her mind reel. A split-second after she'd entered the Portal, she found herself back in the attic. It was just as she'd left it a few minutes earlier—smelling of mold and filled with shadows that even the soft glow from the Portal couldn't dispel.

For a while, she stood there, listening to the street sounds a block away at the perimeter of Old Town, to the wind, whistling around the roof energy units, and the slow creaking of a board somewhere. There was nothing here to alarm her—so why did she feel so reluctant to take the few steps necessary to reach the trapdoor?

With a sigh, she forced herself to move forward, sliding her feet noiselessly over the floorboards. As she lowered the trapdoor, she winced a little at the rasping sound its unoiled hinges made. But before she could drop it into place, two hands appeared at the edges of the opening and then she was staring down into Con-Cord's startled face.

"What are you do'n up there?" he demanded. He swung himself up through the opening, then stood looking around. "What is this place, anyway? And where are your guests?"

Although he sounded more curious than suspicious, AMitY's pulse fluttered with fear. She tried to think of a logical explanation, one he would believe, but nothing came to her. When his eyebrows drew together in a frown, she said the first thing that popped into her mind.

"They've gone back to their swarms. When I was show'n them my sleep 'cove earlier, HUmble discovered the trapdoor in the ceiling. I—I promised to 'ves'gate and tell him what's up here—" She stopped, aware from Cit'zen's tightening jaw that he didn't believe her.

"I've been wait'n in the 'ception hall for the past hour to pay my 'spects to your grandfather. I don't know what's go'n on here, but your guests are still in the house somewhere. Cit'zen frugaLity took it 'pon herself to keep an eye on you. She followed the six of you, saw you go into your sleep 'cove. When you didn't come out, she 'vest'gated, found you were gone. She came to me—which is why I'm here."

It was all AMitY could do not to groan out loud. Behind her, the glow from the window intensified, as if the Portal were reminding her that she had a retreat. As she backed away slowly, she kept her eyes fixed on ConCord. "Cit'zen frugaLity is mistaken," she said. "Or maybe she's try'n to make trouble for me. I 'scorted my friends downstairs mo' than an hour ago."

She had almost reached the window. She groped behind her with one hand, fortified with the knowledge that ConCord couldn't possibly guess her intention. When her hand touched the metal rim of the Portal, which was always so surprisingly warm, she abandoned caution and turned to fling herself through the opening.

But she wasn't quick enough. In an instant, ConCord had reached her and seized her by the arm. "You little fool! Do you think self-term'ation is the answer? Whatev' you've done this time, it can't be that bad. I s'gest you come downstairs to my chambers so we can talk this over calmly."

But AMitY was beyond reason. The fear that she

might be trapped here was too much for her. Frantically, she tried to free herself from ConCord's restraining hand. ConCord gave a smothered oath, then clamped both hands on her shoulders, holding her there. With a cry of despair, she flung herself backward, into the Portal, taking him with her.

There was a queer sensation, as if she were dropping down a long tunnel, a moment of intense cold, another of heat so scorching that it seemed to shrivel her skin. Then she was lying face up in front of the Portal—and next to her, an ignoble heap on the moss, was ConCord's lean body.

XVII

MitY was curled up in the mossy hollow formed by two thick tree roots. The tree that hosted her was called Our Lord Tum'mo by the A'aludes, and unlike most of its kind, it was a solitary tree that had taken root on a rocky slope, high above the valley floor.

Although she'd come here to be alone, to get away from the problems that seemed to proliferate around her like a swarm of insects since her return to E'ewere, she was feeling a little deserted, too. Her former shadows, Dl'lark and Wocho, had become HUmble's constant companions, initiating him into the customs and ways of the A'aludes as they had her earlier.

It seemed ironic to AMitY, now, that she had naively believed that once she got the others here, all their problems would be solved. True, PRudenCe seemed to be recovering from her original shock at the alien ways of the A'aludes—or at least, she had adjusted enough that she would sometimes talk to the small creatures who were so enchanted by her dark hair and gentle manners. She still couldn't bear to be alone, but in time—yes, surely she would learn to appreciate the freedom here as much as she did the food.

That her friend found the A'aludes' crusty bread, the mellow foods her grandfather called butter and cheese, the fruits and berries and sweet cakes, to her liking was apparent from the amount she put away at every meal. And there was no denying that being with Citizen UNison pleased her.

Sometimes, when AMitY saw them sitting together in the small garden behind the guest house, she felt a jealous pang. It was so different with ConCord and her. Out of deference to their hosts, he was polite to her, but there was a chill in his eyes when he looked at her that cut her deeply.

And Citizen UNison? What was PRudenCe's friend really thinking behind those watchful eyes? The A'aludes, who had taken HUmble, Grandfather ausTere and PRudenCe to their hearts so quickly, seemed reluctant to be in UNison's company. In fact, they had a way of drifting away whenever he appeared. She could understand why they avoided Tutu, with her tantrums and her torrents of tears, with her pious lectures and shrill disapproval of their customs, their clothes, even their alien appearance. But what did they sense about UNison that made them avoid him so?

Well, at least, she hadn't made a mistake, bringing her grandfather and HUmble to E'ewere. From the moment the A'aludes had welcomed them, there had been a rapport between the aliens and her relatives. Dl'lark and Wocho had immediately taken HUmble under their wings, and now the three of them were inseparable. At night, they even slept together on the same mound of downy cushions in one corner of the guest house's gathering room—to Tutu's loudly expressed disgust. During the day, they were constantly on the move, exploring the cliff caves, swimming in the brook, helping in the grain fields or the fruit drying yards or scrounging for nuts on the valley slopes.

And Grandfather ausTere, with a whole world of strange flora and fauna to catalog, seemed never to stop. Even though E'ewere's days were a little longer than those of Earth, he begrudged the time he spent eating and sleeping. Surprisingly, he always had time for Lord Som'mos, the pompous Legend Keeper. The two of them spent hours together every day, exchanging information about their respective worlds. Citizen ausTere seemed never to tire of hearing the old A'aludian legends, which naturally endeared him to Lord Som'mos, who never tired of pontificating about the past.

It also surprised AMitY that the A'aludes, who were so leery of UNison, who avoided Tutu at all times, were drawn to ConCord. Although he remained aloof from the small people, as if afraid that he might succumb to their friendliness, they spoke with awe about his determination to return to his own world and whispered about his futile attempts to pass through the Portal.

Since AMitY was smaller than average, the A'aludes must have assumed that all humans were the same size. She suspected that some of their admiration stemmed from ConCord's strength and size. Already some of the A'alude maidens had written ballads about him—

"Queen Aur'ri sent me to find you," ConCord's voice, like an echo of her thoughts, said beside her. "She

1 8 3

tells me that they're afraid the Gra'ack will r'turn."

AMitY's heart twisted a little as she stared up at him. Like the others, he had shed his robe for the soft, close-fitting garments worn by the A'aludes. Under the benevolent rays of E'ewere's sun, his skin had turned dark umber, and his eyes showed specks of gold she hadn't noticed on Earth.

"I like to be 'lone sometimes. I'm sure I'm safe 'nough. I'm too heavy for the Gra'ack to carry off." She hesitate, then added awkwardly, "I'm glad you came. We haven't talked for a long time."

A muscle twitched in ConCord's jawline. "Since you—and, at your orders, HUmble—r'fuse to take me back, there isn't much to say—unless you've changed your mind?"

AMitY shook her head. "If I take you back, even your status won't keep you from be'n questioned 'bout our dis'pearance. Since you won't promise to keep the Portal a secret—" She shrugged.

"How can I promise that? When—*if* I r'turn, I must 'splain my 'volvment in the dis'pearance of five other citizens. If the rest of you r'turn with me, I can say we were in the O'Zones, test'n survival techniques, a prelude to the Outlands expedition. But if we're gone too long or if I r'turn alone, I have no choice but to tell the truth. There's already so much op'sition to the expedition by Code Zealots that the only way I can keep my cred'bil'ty is to vol'teer for a test'n by the Truth machine. So I'm ask'n you 'gain to r'turn us all to Grissom House while there's still time."

This time, AMitY merely shook her head. ConCord's eyes darkened with anger.

"Give it up, AMitY," he said. "Your 'tentions were good, but you must see it won't work. The A'aludes are too kind to tell you that we're disrupt'n their lives and creat'n all kind of dif'culties for them—"

"King L'lando 'vited us here," she said hotly. "They *want* us to live in the valley."

"Are you really so blind that you can't see what a hardship it is for them to feed so many extra people? Haven't you noticed how they avoid Cit'zen UNison— and how he looks at their gold ornaments? Can't you see what Tutu's tantrums and her efforts to impose her own standards 'pon their culture is do'n to these people you call your friends?"

"They *are* my friends! And Tutu will change. We've only been here a few days—she just doesn't un'stand yet that the A'aludes have their own way of do'n th'n's."

"She won't change—but the A'aludes might. Fanatics can be ver' persuasive. She's been 'doct'nated with the worst aspects of the Code all her life. I've seen these products of the School for Illegals 'fore. They keep the Court'sy Guard busy with their c'plaints 'gainst other cit'zens. Yest'day, I saw Tutu down by the stream harang'n a group of A'alude youngsters 'cause they were swim'n nude."

"They pay no 'tention to her. They laugh when she quotes the Code to them, 'specially the ones 'bout not touch'n or laugh'n in public."

"Are you so sure? One by one, without look'n at each other, the children dressed and left. She's bring'n shame to these gentle people, us'n the Code just as fanatics and Zealots have always used their laws to 'flict their b'liefs on other cultures."

"I'll talk to her 'gain. She doesn't un'stand mind-talk or realize how painful her bursts of temper are to the A'aludes—"

"And give her 'nother weapon to use 'gainst them? You must see that there's no other choice but to r'turn her—to r'turn *all* of us to Earth."

"If we r'turn, my grandfather will be sent back to the Termine Swarms. I thought you liked him—do you want to see him stagnate in a Termine ward? Haven't you seen how happy he is here? And HUmble—do you really think he could 'just to the r'strictions of his school now that he's had a taste of freedom? And what 'bout PRudenCe? I know you're fond of her. She turned sixteen four days ago—do you want her to be ster'lized?"

ConCord's eyes didn't waver. "And UNison? Not only hasn't he lifted a finger to do any work since he got here, but he spent so much time hang'n 'round the goldsmiths' cave that they finally stopped work and took a hol'day. He asks far too many questions 'bout the source of the A'aludes's gold—and the location of their treas'ry."

"All the mo' reason why he should stay here," she argued. "How would we keep him from talk'n 'bout the gold? And what if the author'ties force HUmble and me to bring a squad of Barrier Guards through the Portal to raid the A'aludes' treas'ry?"

ConCord was silent for a moment. "Then you and HUmble stay here. The two of you can't disrupt the A'aludes' way of life or put too much of a drain on their food supplies."

Again, AMitY maintained a stubborn silence. ConCord studied her stiff face a few moments before he said, "I could make it worth UNison's while to r'main quiet 'bout the gold. The senior stewart at Grissom House is near Termine age. I can offer UNison the 'signment. It's a mid-status job. I'm sure it would buy his silence."

"And what 'bout PRudenCe? You know what will happen to her if she r'turns."

"There are ways to circumvent the Code, 'specially since her case is borderline. 'Ceptions can be made. And I'm sure that she'd gladly trade E'ewere, which I doubt she'll ever really 'just to, to life in the fam'ly swarms as UNison's bondmate. I can even 'range for a 'mestic 'signment for her."

He was silent for a moment before he added, "As for your grandfather, he doesn't have to r'turn to the Termine wards. I can promise him a place in my expedition, where his knowledge of biology would be ver' useful. I think, if you talk to him, you'll find he agrees with all I've said. Don't you see, AMitY, that the expedition might be the only chance our people have to stave off the disaster of intol'ble overcrowd'n? How can we turn our backs on them?"

In his urgency, he reached out and touched her arm. His hand, warm from the sun, seemed to burn her skin as he went on. "For Harmony's sake, AMitY, open your eyes! We can't take our pers'nal happ'ness at the 'spense of the A'aludes. Ask yourself why there haven't been any gather'n's since the one that first night—and while you're at it, ask yourself why Princess Gw'wanna and Lord Tor'ro have postponed their bond'n cer'mony so long."

AMitY discovered that she'd lost the power of speech. She wanted to repudiate his words, but she was suddenly remembering the sadness she'd noticed so often in Gw'wanna's eyes. And there were other things—the amounts of food all of them—especially HUmble, with his voracious appetite, and PRudenCe, with her sweet tooth—managed to pack away at every meal. And UNison—no wonder he made her uneasy.

The thing she saw in his eyes when he looked at the A'aludes' gold was greed. . . .

"You see it now, don't you? You know I'm right. Give it up and take the four of us back through the Portal."

ConCord's voice was soft; he was so close that she could feel his warm breath on her face. But instead of disarming her, she felt a deep hurt. Because what he was really saying was that he wanted to leave her, that he was perfectly willing for her to stay behind.

She jerked her hand away and stood up. In her anger, she lashed out at him, using her tongue as a weapon.

"You talk 'bout fanatics and Zealots, but isn't that exactly what you are, Cit'zen ConCord? You have one idea in your head, and that's all that matters to you. Oh, you're ver' persuasive, but you've 'ready warned me 'bout fanatics, haven't you? So you're wast'n your time. It'll take a while, but Tutu will come 'round and PRudenCe will 'just to the life here and UNison will see that he must do his share of the work."

She looked him straight in the eye. "And you'll come 'round, too, or you'll be a ver' unhappy for the rest of your life. 'Cause I'll never change my mind about tak'n you back—never!"

XVIII

MitY was walking along the banks of Our Lord Tok'ko, on her way back to the guest house, when she heard a low humming. Her spirits lifted a little when she realized it was Dl'lark. He was sitting on a huge slab of rock, his bare feet dangling over the sparkling water of the brook. Absorbed in watching a school of tiny, blue-striped fish, he was humming one of his mother's songs to himself—or maybe, AMitY thought, he was entertaining his brothers, the fish.

She looked around for her brother and Wocho, knowing they would be nearby, and saw that they were curled up in a thick patch of the moss-grass a few feet away, both of them sound asleep.

At Dl'lark's wave, she joined him on the rock, and for a while they sat in companionable silence, watching the fish. AMitY spoke first. "Are any of the other children the same age as you and Lord Wocho?" she asked idly.

"We were the only ones born that sun-cycle—or for two sun-cycles before and after," Dl'lark told her. "I was born first and then Wocho came a few days later. If it weren't. for Lord Dl'lark and Lady Ga'amina, he would be much younger than I."

AMitY stared at him. "I don't un'stand. Who are they—and what did they have to do with Lord Wocho's age?"

"They are the ones Wocho and I replaced. No one had taken last-flight for several sun-cycles, so of course there could be no new births," Dl'lark explained. "Although my parents—and Wocho's parents—had drawn the white feathers at the birth lotteries, they had been waiting a long time. Then Lord Dl'lark, who tended the—what your grandfather calls sheep, fell from the rocks and passed, and a week later, Lady Ga'amina, who was very old, grew tired of life and decided to take last-flight into the Wild Wood. That's why Wocho and I were born only a few days apart. It is very good to have a ménage-mate. Most are not so lucky."

He paused, his head to one side. "My mother calls. She is helping Lady Hon'no bake today's bread. Since you take such interest in the old skills, she asks if you would like to join her." He slid off the rock. "I'll go with you. Maybe she'll give me a tart for Cit'zen HUmble, who has such a taste for them."

Although AMitY rose and followed Dl'lark to the baker's shop, her mind was still on the interrupted conversation. Did Dl'lark mean that no new children could be born to an A'aludian couple until another citizen terminated—and then only if the couple had won the right in a lottery?

ConCord had told her to open her eyes, to ask herself why there hadn't been a gathering since the night she'd returned to E'ewere—and also to ask herself why Princess Gw'wanna and Lord Tor'ro had postponed their bonding so long. Had he guessed that these people, seemingly so free of laws and restrictions, were just as custom-bound by their traditions as her own people? Was he so much more observant than she—or was it because he was less willing to deliberately close his eyes to Truth?

Although she was deeply troubled by her own questions, AMitY waited until Dl'lark had talked the baker's wife out of a fruit tart for HUmble's sweet tooth and had left to join his friends before she asked Queen Aur'ri to explain her son's words.

"There is food for only so many and no more," Queen Aur'ri said. "When one passes, then another can be born. This is our way."

And what about guests? AMitY thought. *Is it your way to provide food for them by postponing new births—and, sometimes, as in Gw'wanna's case, new bondings?*

Since it was a question she couldn't politely ask, instead she said, "Couldn't you sow mo' grain, plant mo' vegetables and 'large your orchards—and maybe c'struct art'ficial ponds where alissi could be grown? And surely, there's plenty of graz'n land for mo' milk beasts."

"But then we would deprive our friends, the fish and birds and wild animals, of their food and homes." Queen Aur'ri's voice was patient, as if she were explaining a puzzle to a child. "In his wisdom, the Old One marked out the fields that were to be ours. To encroach upon the land of others would be wrong. Sometimes, I admit, our ways are difficult"—her eyes strayed to the other side of the kitchen where her daughter, Princess Gw'wanna, was helping the baker's wife sift flour for more bread—"but we must follow the Old One's directives. It is best not to think of other ways lest they tempt us."

AMitY digested this as she watched Queen Aur'ri knead the pungent bread dough; her hands were surprisingly strong as she expertly slapped and turned the spongy mixture.

"Prince Dl'lark spoke of one of your elders who went into the Wild Wood so Wocho's parents could have a child," AMitY said. "Is this another of your customs?"

"No, not a custom. But it *is* an act of great kindness. Lady Ga'amina was very old. She suffered from the infirmities that come with age. Her life had lost its savor since the passing of her life-mate—and Lord Wocho's parents had been waiting so long for a child. In her compassion, she decided to make last-flight into the Wild Wood so a child could be born to them before they grew too old."

"It seems so—sad," AMitY said.

"Sad? But it was a happy event! Lady Ga'amina had lived a good life, although she'd never drawn the white feather at the birth lotteries. Even so, she gave life to Wocho by choosing to take last-flight early. She stayed with us long enough to be the first to hold young Wocho in her arms, as was her right. If he had been a girl, he would have been given her name, as my son was given the name of Lord Dl'lark, the herdsmaster, whose passing permitted *his* birth. So Lady Ga'amina is to be envied, not pitied. She will be honored in our songs for a long time."

She paused to study AMitY's troubled face. "Perhaps, if your own people had such traditions, there would not be the overcrowding on your world that you describe."

AMitY had a sudden vision of the sleeping bays,

the shuffling throngs, the privacy cowls that hid the faces of citizens from each other. She thought of the stifling sameness, the incessant noise, the tasteless, unchanging diet, and she knew that Queen Aur'ri was right.

So why did she feel so defensive, as if she wanted to justify a way of life that she, of all people, knew to be oppressive? Was it because she had finally been forced to realize that the lives of the A'aludes, for all that it was more pleasant than that of her own people, were just as custom-bound and restricted?

As she always did when she had problems too knotty to solve on her own, AMitY sought out her grandfather.

She found him in the guest house's small storage room, which he had taken over as a workshop. He was bending over a low table, so intent upon his examination of an assortment of plants and seeds that he didn't notice her entrance.

Since the A'aludes, without a written language, had no need for paper, her grandfather had improvised his own. Laboriously, he took down his notes on silk remnants, stretched over twig frames, using berry juice for ink and a feather quill for a pen.

As AMitY studied his absorbed face, as unlined as a much younger man's, her determination not to be swayed by the information she'd just learned was reinforced. To return this man, with his questing mind, to the stagnation of a Termine ward was unthinkable— and yet, how many hundreds of thousands of citizens like her grandfather were trapped in those dreary wards with nothing to keep their minds from deteriorating? If ConCord's expedition succeeded in opening up new lands and resources to her people, other Termines would be freed from their prisons, just as her grandfather had been.

She shook her head, repudiating the thought. What assurance did she have that ConCord's trip into the Outlands would materialize? There were so many factors against it, not the least of them being the Zealots on the Council of Nine. It would be two years before ConCord assumed his father's place on the board; in the meantime, she only had ConCord's promise that her grandfather wouldn't be returned to the Termine Swarms. . . .

Citizen ausTere looked up and gave AMitY an absent smile. "Come look at this, AMitY," he said, holding up a broad, flat leaf. " 'Less my mem'ry's at fault, this is ver' much like one of our own ginkgo trees. They're 'stinct in N'York, so I've never seen one, but from what I 'member from books, the 'semblance is 'mark'ble."

He pointed to a dainty, pale yellow flower. "I've seen this spec'men 'fore—in the State Conserv'tory. It's common name is primrose, and they once grew wild in Old Europe—and still might, for all I know. And those black birds that're so pesky in the grain fields? I'm sure those are rooks, also indig'nous to Europe. So the question is—how did they find their way into E'ewere?"

Despite AMitY's own pressing problems, her grandfather's excitement was contagious. She studied the yellow flower curiously. "Have you asked Lord Som'mos about this, grandfather?"

"Yes—but too much time has passed since the A'aludes first came here. The sheer volume of legends means that the old ones are grad'ally lost—which is one of the problems with a culture that has no written language and has to d'pend on oral history. Even so, it's Lord Som'mos's b'lief that the Old One brought the animals and plants here just as he b'lieves their mentor created the valley 'spec'ally for them."

"Is that pos'ble?"

"Not by any technol'gy known on Earth, but—yes, the Old One could've brought plants and an'mals from Earth—or any other world the Portal touches. Some of the trees and plants, 'clud'n the legumes the A'aludes cult'vate, are unlike an'th'n I've ever seen or read 'bout. Most are prob'ly indig'nous to E'ewere, but others may well be from other worlds, 'clud'n our own Earth."

He rubbed his hands together briskly, smiling. "Well, as our good Keeper of Legends would say—it's a myst'ry, all right. And there are other myst'ries, such as the A'aludes' 'mestic an'mals, which are so much like our own goats and sheep. It's hard to 'lieve that two planets, in dif'rent solar systems—or even in dif'rent d'mensions—could have parallel ev'lution, but 'course it could happen."

"The day I came to E'ewere, a leaf blew through the Portal. That's how I knew it was real. Could the r'verse be true? Could seeds and an'mals from Earth find their way into E'ewere through the Portal?"

"It's pos'ble, I 'spose." But Citizen ausTere's voice held doubt.

"We weren't the only aliens to come through the Portal," AMitY reminded him. "Why not seeds and an'mals? We know the Gra'ack and Our Lady Sab'bri came from other worlds."

"You speak Truth. But both are highly 'volved life-forms. To be able to pass through the Portal, they must have wave patterns on the par with humans, which cert'ly points to 'tell'gence."

1 9 5

"But what of the leaf the wind blew through the Portal?"

"Ah, that must've been a 'ducement to lure you 'way from danger. You tell me that the dreams and visions of E'ewere came more often after you were sent to the Common Swarms. If the Portal is 'tuned to your brainwave pattern, as I s'pect, then its primary d'rective might be to p'tect you—and others like you—from harm. And if it sensed your disHarmony, which was very strong at the time, then perhaps it made E'ewere 'vailable to you as a refuge. If the Portal was used for 'sploration, surely there would be a built-in safety factor so it would be 'med'ately 'vail'ble to any 'splorer who might need to make a quick retreat."

He tapped his fingertips together, his eyes introspective. "What in'lect'al giants the Portal's creators were! It's a marvel of technol'gy, far beyond anyth'n we humans have ever been able to create, even in pre-Chaos times."

"Then you think the Portal's creators are 'stinct?"

"Oh, I'm sure they must be. The Portal is obv'ously a relic, created by some un'mag'ably 'vanced race of be'n's who conquered space only to be conquered 'emselves by—what? An even mo' 'vanced race? Or did they 'volve beyond the need for machines—or simply grow old and term'nate, as all th'n's do, even galaxies. One th'n I'm sure of: the Portal wasn't built by the ancestors of the A'aludes. There isn't a trace of technol'gy, not even the wheel, in their culture, as there would be if they were su'vivors of such a race."

"Is it pos'ble that the Old One created the Portal?"

"Anyth'n's pos'ble. Or he—I'm assum'n his kind

has gender—could be the last of the race who built the Portal."

"If the Portal is so old, you wonder why it still works, don't you?" AMitY said.

"Why indeed? Was it act'vated ac'dently by some pass'n creature on one of the worlds it touches? Was it forgotten in some ancient crisis or mass 'vacuation? And why, if the threat of the Troggo is so fearful, didn't the Old One simply turn if off?"

AMitY felt a small chill. "Maybe it *can't* be turned off."

Citizen ausTere regarded her with bright eyes, his head tilted to one side like an inquisitive bird. "Int'rest'n premise. It could be that to turn it off, once it was act'vated, would disrupt the fabric of the un'verse. Or maybe it was left on as a means of r'treat. There are many myst'ries here, and our friends, the A'aludes, are prob'bly wise not to worry 'bout them. Even so, I'd like to take a closer look at the Portal, 'spec'ly at that intrigu'n dome. Perhaps—yes, I think it's time I took a trip back up the knoll. And ver' soon, too."

The sudden grimness in his voice startled AMitY. "You think there's still some danger c'nected with the Portal? Surely, the Troggo is dead by now, even if it isn't just a myth."

"Oh, I doubt it's a myth. If the Old One, who seems to be incred'bly long-lived, believes the Troggo is still a danger to the A'aludes—and in fact to all of E'ewere—then it's someth'n to be taken ser'ously." He paused, as if considering a new possibility. "I do wonder, though, why it hasn't come 'fore now?"

"Maybe it did. And maybe it was trapped in

'nother world," AMitY said, remembering her glimpses of alien worlds, none so hospitable to humankind as E'ewere—or Earth.

Her grandfather gave a fretful sigh. "So many mys'ries—such as the one 'volv'n the Sojourner. Who was he? From what era of our past did he come? If the legends are correct, he was Caucasian—or at least, his beard was fair, his eyes blue. We know he spoke pre-Chaos English—did he come from Old America or from Old Britain? Was he a soldier—or simply a cit'zen caught up in one of the old wars?"

"Whoever he was, he must have kept quiet 'bout E'ewere—or else nobody b'lieved his stories."

Citizen ausTere leaned back on his stool and rubbed his eyes. "I wonder how many of Earth's old myths come from the tales brought back from trav'lers who, like the Sojourner, vis'ted the valley so long ago that the mem'ry of them has been lost from A'aludian legends? There's a quality 'bout the A'aludes that reminds me of fairies—"

"Fairies? What's that?"

"It's an obsolete word. They were winged creatures, part of the old myths that one of our Councils, in their wisdom, 'bolished, 'long with other s'perfl'ous th'n's like science fiction." There was a familiar dryness in his voice that made AMitY smile. "It's pos'ble those myths were d'rived from stories earlier trav'lers took back to Earth with them, stories that were distorted by time like the tales of Marco Polo once were."

The clatter of feet outside the door interrupted AMitY. She exchanged smiles with her grandfather, knowing they were about to be invaded by HUmble and his friends.

But when HUmble came into the room he was alone.

"Where are your friends?" AMitY asked.

"They went to a gather'n. Several of the elders are go'n on a trip. The whole village went to see them off. I would've gone, too, only the high valley's in'cess'ble if you don't have wings." HUmble's usually cheerful face was glum as he added, "It must be top-o, hav'n wings."

AMitY nodded absently. "Did Prince Dl'lark tell you where the elders were go'n?"

"Into the Wild Wood, he said." He heaved a deep sigh. "It's not much fun 'thout them."

Involuntarily, AMitY looked at her grandfather. From the expression on his face, she knew that he, too, had caught the significance of HUmble's words. Did this mean that some of the elders had decided to terminate themselves so that couples waiting for children could have them? But why at *this* particular time, just when the harvest was so good?

"—wish he'd stop bother'n us. He's always try'n to talk me into tak'n him back through the Portal," HUmble was saying. At her startled look, his face turned pink. "I know we must r'spect our elders, but—well, he's always ask'n Dl'lark and Wocho questions 'bout the treas'ry and try'n to find out where the gold mines are and ask'n me to take him back through the Portal."

"Are you talk'n 'bout Cit'zen ConCord?" AMitY said.

He gave her a disgusted look. " 'Course not. *He* knows I can't go 'gainst your wishes. Weren't you listen'n, sister? It's Cit'zen UNison. He got Dl'lark to take him to the treas'ry to see the gold, and now he's act'n ver' strange. Fact is, ev'body been act'n termy, 'clud'n

Cit'zen Tutu. Ev'th'n here Offends her. She's sure she's go'n to term'ate just 'cause she hasn't had her Panacea this month. She says the A'aludes are Decadent for laugh'n in public and touch'n each other so much, and she c'plains 'cause there's no sani-stalls or sonic-fresh'ners or holovision."

He stopped, his expression wistful. "I miss books, myself. I offered to teach Dl'lark and Wocho how to read and write, but they thought I was mak'n a joke." He looked away, avoiding AMitY's eyes. "I've been think'n that maybe I could sneak back to Grissom House dur'n Third Time when ev'body's sleep'n and borrow some of the books from Cit'zen ConCord's library. I could get some slates and chalk for you, Grandfather asuTere, and some games and—"

"Is this Cit'zen ConCord's idea?" AMitY said.

Her brother shook his head, but before he could answer her question, Citizen ausTere, his voice unusually abrupt, interrupted. "I want you to run an errand for me, grandson. Find Cit'zen ConCord and tell him I must see him right 'way."

HUmble helped himself to a piece of fruit, blithely ignoring the fact that it was one of his grandfather's specimens, before he went whistling off, a practice he'd picked up from his A'alude friends. Confronted by a new worry, AMitY's throat tightened as she watched him.

What would happen when the newness of E'ewere wore off and there was nothing more to learn about the valley or the A'aludes? Would HUmble, with his insatiable curiosity, become restless and do something dangerous—like slipping back through the Portal to bring books and games and other diversions into E'ewere?

And on the other hand, so far Dl'lark and Wocho

had been patient with HUmble's limitations; but wasn't it a little like a sighted person deliberately putting on a blindfold so he wouldn't have an advantage over a blind friend? How long would their patience last before they returned to the sky, leaving HUmble behind on the ground?

AMitY realized that her grandfather had been silent for a long time. She looked up and caught him watching her. From the compassion on his face, she wondered if he had picked up the A'aludes' gift for reading minds.

"I'd like to take 'nother look at the Portal—and the Sojourner's message," he said. "With the A'aludes busy with their own affairs, this might be the best time. I'll need some help clear'n 'way the moss so I'm go'n to ask Cit'zen ConCord to come 'long. I think the time has come to—"

He broke off, and when he went on, it was on a different track. "In fact, I think we should all go. We've been so busy this past week that we haven't really had a chance to talk. Why don't you find PRudenCe and UNison and enlist their help in p'suad'n Cit'zen Tutu to come, too?"

"She'll probably throw 'nother tantrum when she sees the Portal," AMitY said doubtfully. "If you feel we need a meet'n, why can't we talk here? I'm sure Cit'zen ConCord won't want to be in my comp'ny—"

"But *I* do. Now run along, Granddaughter. Cit'zens PRudenCe and UNison are prob'ly in the garden—and I'm sure I saw Citizen Tutu in the gather'n room earlier."

Hiding her doubts, AMitY bowed and left the shed. She found PRudenCe and UNison in the small garden behind the guest house, sitting on a stone bench.

UNison was talking earnestly to PRudenCe, using his hands to emphasize his words, and it seemed to AMitY that his eyes had a hot, dry look, as if he had a fever.

When he looked up and saw her, he fell silent, his expression wary, and something she hadn't allowed herself to think until this moment flashed through her mind.

I don't like you and I don't trust you, Cit'zen UNison....

"Cit'zen ausTere wants us to go with him to the Portal," she said. "He needs help clearing off the moss so he can read the Sojourner's message."

"Why doesn't he get the A'aludes to help him?" UNison's tone bordered on rudeness. *"He* seems to be in the creatures' good graces."

"They've gone to a gather'n and aren't 'vail'ble. 'Sides, Cit'zen ausTere thinks it's time we had a meet'n of our own."

UNison's sandy eyebrows rose. He was silent a moment, as if weighing her words. "Ver' well—but you might have trouble talk'n Cit'zen Tutu into leav'n the guest house. She's sulk'n 'cause Queen Aur'ri asked her to stop scold'n the children." He gave PRudenCe a sidelong look. "You'd better go with Cit'zen AMitY, PRudenCe. I have someth'n' to do first. I'll meet you at the Portal."

PRudenCe rose so quickly that AMitY wondered if she and UNison had quarreled. As they walked back to the guest house, she studied her friend surreptiously. The pink tunic and trousers PRudenCe wore were becoming to her dark hair and her sepia-colored skin, and her face seemed subtly to have filled out in the past few days—but why did she always seem so depressed lately? When was the last time she'd heard PRudenCe laugh?

What had happened to her friend's irrepressible high spirits, her irreverent little jokes?

"Are you happy here, PRudenCe?" she asked abruptly.

PRudenCe hesitated before she said, "I'm ver' grateful you 'cluded me—and UNison. But it's—well, scary here, all the empty space, I mean. And it'll take a little time, get'n used to—to the A'aludes and their ways." She gave a shaky laugh. "No matter *what* Tutu says, I don't really b'lieve the A'aludes are Hedonists even if they do have loose—unOrthodox ways. I think that when they realize how some of the th'n's they do Offend us, they'll change, don't you?"

"No, I don't," AMitY said tightly. She wanted to say more, but the droop at the corners of PRudenCe's mouth stopped her. Suddenly, she felt years older than her friend. Would PRudenCe *really* get used to E'ewere in time—or was she secretly regretting that she'd agreed so readily to come along? Another, even more disturbing question came to her. Was it possible that PRudenCe, who had never felt any desire to be alone, would have been much happier in the Sterie Swarms?

The question was troubling, as so many things were these days. Now, just when she should be so happy, she couldn't seem to stop thinking about the coolness in ConCord's eyes when he looked at her, or of the difficult adjustments that lay ahead for them all.

It had been so much simpler before she'd achieved her goal, AMitY reflected . . . and so much easier when she'd been so sure she knew just who her enemy was.

XIX

hey found Tutu in the gathering room of the guest house. Characteristically, she had scorned the piles of soft floor pillows and was sitting on the stone floor—her feet tucked up inside her robe, her arms wrapped around her legs, her small pointed chin resting on her knees.

Unlike the others, she had refused to wear the comfortable garments that the A'aludes had so generously furnished them, and her robe, which she wore even when she slept, was wrinkled and frayed around the hem. In the shadow of her privacy cowl, her face had a forlorn look, and unexpectedly AMitY felt a stirring of sympathy for the girl.

After all, like ConCord, Tutu had been dragged through the Portal against her will, leaving behind the only life she'd ever known—and one for which she seemed uncommonly suited. And what did she have in exchange? An alien people with ways she had been taught were Hedonistic, a world that held none of the amenities or diversions she was used to—and a future that promised more of the same.

Tutu looked up, and a scowl settled over her face.

AMitY sighed inwardly. Even with PRudenCe's help, it was doubtful she could persuade Tutu to go up the knoll with the others. Tutu, with her deceptively angelic look, her pious words—and her iron will—was not one to follow orders from those she suspected of being Hedonists.

But to AMitY's surprise, when she relayed her grandfather's request, Tutu hesitated only a moment before she got up, pulled her cowl down and adjusted her belt pouch. "Ver' well, I'll go 'long," she said ungraciously.

It was a silent party that climbed the steep slopes of the knoll. Both Citizen ausTere and ConCord carried knapsacks made of A'aludian wool, but AMitY was too apathetic to ask what was inside the bulky bundles. Her grandfather seemed lost in his own thoughts, and ConCord was obviously disinclined to talk, even when HUmble, perpetually hungry, asked him if the knapsacks contained food for a picnic.

HUmble, still looking glum, stopped frequently to look upward, as if expecting to see his friends wheeling overhead. Only Tutu seemed to be in good spirits. Taking in her small, secret smile, AMitY wondered if she were drawing some perverse pleasure from the general gloom.

When they reached the top of the knoll, Citizen ausTere turned off HUmble's questions with a brusque, "Let's wait for Citizen UNison to join us."

He turned his attention to the small dome-shaped protrusion in the frame of the Portal. When ConCord joined him, AMitY felt an unexpected pang of jealousy at the obvious rapport between the two men.

She turned her back on them and stared down into the valley. At the bottom of the knoll, UNison was just starting his climb. As he drew closer, she saw that he was carrying a large square of silk, knotted into a pouch. From the way the material sagged, its content was very heavy, and she watched him curiously, only half-listening to the two men behind her.

"—obv'ously a device that controls the Portal's functions, an energy field of some sort. But it's unlike anyth'n I've ever heard of or read 'bout," her grandfather was saying. "The technol'gy necessary to create a matter converter would be beyond the need of levers or switches or conduits. I suspect it was op'rated by pure thought."

"AMitY and HUmble seem to be in accord with the Portal—do you think they could learn to op'rate it?" ConCord asked.

"With proper train'n, perhaps. The variants would be infinite—it would be immensely dang'rous. In fact, there would have to be a built-in safety mechanism— what our ancestors called a fail-safe device—a way to turn it off. I wonder if—"

"Well, Senior Cit'zen ausTere, what's this all 'bout?" It was UNison. His face was flushed from his climb, and when he let the bundle he was carrying slip to the ground, he put one foot on it as if expecting someone to snatch it away. "It was a long trek up that hill. I hope it's someth'n 'portant."

There was something false about his jovial tone. Citizen ausTere must have sensed it, too, because he gave the younger man a long, thoughtful look. "I do have someth'n 'portant to d'cuss with all of you—but first, I want to take a closer look at the writ'n 'bove the Portal." He turned back to ConCord. "It'll take two of us to clear away the moss."

"Leave that to your grandson and me." ConCord beckoned to HUmble. "Climb up on my shoulders—and you'll need someth'n to clear the moss off with."

After HUmble found a stick, he put his foot into ConCord's cupped hands and, with his usual apomb, climbed up, looking very pleased with the attention he was getting. In the amber light, his hair had a ruddier tone than it did on Earth, and his eyes sparkled with mischief as he grinned down at AMitY and gave her a mock bow, almost losing his balance in the process.

He began cleaning off the thick accumulation of moss from the stones. As the characters came clear, AMitY realized they had the shape of familiar letters. Although HUmble had started from right to left, she recognized a word, then another, but her mind refused to acknowledge their meaning. It was only when she heard PRudenCe's gasp that she reluctantly stood back and read the message written on the stones.

"Beware of Man, for *he* is the Troggo."

For a long moment, she stared at the Sojourner's message, refusing to accept its significance; and then her defenses went down and she was assaulted by ugly images:

The seething masses of citizens on even the least traveled of N'York's streets.

Tutu's pious exhortations to the A'aludes on the virtues of the Code and their own Hedonism.

The greed on UNison's face when he looked at the A'aludes' gold.

The vast amounts of fruit and bread and vegetables that HUmble and PRudenCe, that all of them, consumed at every meal.

The A'alude elders, who were making their last flight into the Wild Wood today—not so more A'aludian children could be born, but so there would be food enough to feed their unwanted guests.

Her own duplicity.

She sank down on the spongy moss, and because she didn't have her privacy cowl to hide behind, she buried her face in her hands. When she felt a touch on her shoulder, she looked up and saw that it was ConCord who was kneeling beside her. Not since they'd arrived had he looked at her without censure in his eyes, but now his eyes were so filled with compassion that instinctively AMitY leaned against him, pressing her face against his arm.

"I don't un'stand." PRudenCe's voice held bewilderment. "Surely, the Sojourner didn't mean . . ." Her words trailed off.

When no one answered her unspoken question, AMitY pushed herself away from ConCord and looked up at her friend.

"Earth must have been the place where the A'aludes settled after their homeworld became uninhab'able," she said wearily. "Their world, like Earth, must've been one of the planets the Portal touched on."

She was silent a moment, remembering a planet of ice and cold with a dying sun that she'd caught a glimpse of during one of her trips through the Portal. Had that been the A'alude's homeworld?

"So they came to Earth," she went on. "And then our ancestors drove them out, and they took refuge on E'ewere. Now they guard the Portal—but it has been so long that, when the Troggo finally 'peared, they no longer rec'nized their ancient en'my."

Citizen ausTere nodded. "And that's why the A'aludes resemble our old myths of winged fairies and elves, and why so many of the valley plants and an'mals are the same. When the A'aludes took refuge here, millenniums ago, they brought along seed and cut'n's of Earth plants and trees and their 'mestic an'mals, perhaps even a few pets, which 'came the 'cestors of the rooks."

AMitY weighed the lack of surprise in his voice. "You s'pected this all 'long, didn't you?"

"I wasn't sure—not till now. The Sojourner, who must've been a man of compassion, carved a warning there, not for the A'aludes, who have no written language, but for any human who might come through the Portal. Perhaps he did warn the A'aludes, too. If so, the warn'n's been forgotten."

"Well, *we* know the truth now—and we have no choice but to r'turn to our own world," ConCord said quietly. "We've done 'nough damage to the A'aludes, disrupt'n their lives, ravag'n their food supplies, mak'n it nec'sary for their elders to term'nate themselves in order to feed us—"

"But they didn't *say* anyth'n," HUmble burst out. His face was so pale that his freckles stood out like tiny grains of sand across his nose. "Why didn't they say someth'n, Grandfather ausTere? I would've eaten less!"

"The food is the least of it. The real danger is the human birthrate. Cit'zens PRudenCe and UNison, AMitY and ConCord, and in time, Young Cit'zen Tutu and you, grandson, would bond and have children, and your children would have children and 'ven'ually, humans would push out the A'aludes, and we would turn this peaceful, fragile place into a replica of the one we left."

"But we wouldn't have to stay in the valley," HUmble said eagerly. "We could settle somewhere else on E'ewere. Maybe the Old One the A'aludes talk 'bout would create a place for us the way he did for them."

"He would put the same r'strictions on our birth-rate as he did the A'aludes, but can you be sure that those who follow us would honor those r'strictions? When, in all the his'ry of mankind, have we ever been able to control our pop'lation 'cept through famine, war, or pest'lence? We would mult'ply and spread out over E'ewere, turn'n it into a wasteland. And that's why we must r'turn to Earth—'fore it's too late."

He laid a gentle hand on AMitY's head. "You know I speak Truth, don't you AMitY? It was a lovely dream, but now it's ended. We must go back—and as soon as pos'ble. If we leave now, there'll still be time to save the A'alude elders who have gone into the Wild Wood today."

AMitY's mind moved sluggishly, turning over his words. "But if we go back—are you sure we can keep the Portal a secret? How can we avoid the questions of the Guard—and the Truth Committee?" She turned in time to catch a secret smile on Tutu's face. "Cit'zen Tutu, for one, would c'sider it her duty to betray the A'aludes."

"If the son of the Chief Arb'trator says he took a group of citizens on a week's trek into the O'Zone as a 'sper'mint to see how they'd s'vive, I doubt anyone'd challenge him," Citizen ausTere said drily. "As for Cit'zen Tutu—she should c'sider the 'vantages of hav'n the patronage of a future Arb'trator. I don't think she would 'joy the life of a Sterie. I un'stand the Sterie Swarms are quite Hedonistic."

Tutu gave him a sullen look, but AMitY knew that she would remain quiet—in her own self-interest.

"And UNison?" she said. "What if he decides it's to *his* best interests to tell 'bout the A'aludes' gold? If they sent us 'fore the Truth machines, the whole story will come out. They could force me—or HUmble—to r'turn to E'ewere with a squad of Barrier Guards by threaten'n to term'nate you, Grandfather."

It was ConCord who answered her. "Cit'zen UNison is an ambitious man, AMitY." UNison sucked in an Offended breath, and ConCord paused to give him a hard look. "There are doors I can open for him that will far outweigh any temp'rary 'vantage of betray'n the A'aludes. And I've already promised you that PRudenCe will never 'come a Sterie. As for Cit'zen ausTere"—his voice softened—"his knowledge of biol'gy will be needed on the expedition. Your brother's energy would be an asset, too. How 'bout it, HUmble—would you like to go 'splor'n in the Outlands?"

HUmble cast one last look upward. "Let's go," he said cheerfully.

UNison had a strange look in his eyes. Even before he spoke, AMitY knew he would accept ConCord's proposal.

"I'll hold you to your promise, Cit'zen ConCord," he said, and to her ears, the words sounded like a threat.

"What about AMitY?" PRudenCe demanded. "She's giv'n up the most. Do you have any treats in your belt pouch for *AMitY*, Cit'zen ConCord?"

ConCord hesitated briefly. "She's ver' welcome to come on the expedition, too," he said softly.

AMitY met the warmth in his eyes and knew that he was offering her something more than a place on the expedition. Without answering the question in his eyes, she turned and looked at the shadows lengthening over the valley, at the amber sun, so benign and so beloved, just dropping out of sight on the opposite side of the valley.

She would miss E'ewere. There would be times when she would grieve for it, yearn for its peace and solitude. No matter how busy she became in a life that looked to be exciting and rewarding now, she would always remember how E'ewere's sun gilded the edges of the trees at this time of day. . . .

Resolutely, she turned her back on the valley and held out her hand to ConCord. "You'd better go first. I left the trapdoor open, after all. By now, they must have d'covered the attic room."

t took such a short time to get them all through the Portal that AMitY felt a little let down. It seemed wrong, somehow, that such an important decision, one that had caused her so much soul-searching and pain, should end up being almost prosaic. As she stood by the window, willing the amber glow of E'ewere to fade, she wondered if the ancient race who had created the Portal had become blasé about it eventually, moving from one alien world to another with no more fanfare than a citizen of her own world passing through the traffic lanes on one of N'York's busy streets.

From the grayness of the light that came through the window, it was another overcast day in N'York. Already, the others looked different. The pallid light drained the color from their wool tunics and turned their tanned skins sallow. All of them, even Tutu, were sober-faced, as if reality had suddenly laid its cold hand upon them. Was it the inevitable questions that lay ahead that made ConCord look so grim and her grandfather seem so much older suddenly? Was HUmble, whose young face was so pale, just beginning to realize what he'd lost: the freedom, the companionship, the joy of E'ewere?

And PRudenCe—why did she keep watching UNison, almost as if she expected him to explode any minute? Even UNison, usually so pragmatic, had the feverish look in his eyes that she'd seen there before. For the first time, she noticed that he was still clinging to his bundle.

"What do you have there?" ConCord, too, had noticed UNison's packet.

"It's my robe and sandals," UNison said quickly. "I had a 'spicion we'd be going back so—"

"Nonsense, Cit'zen UNison," Citizen ausTere interrupted. He gestured toward the two bundles at his own feet. "Your robe is here. Cit'zen ConCord and I brought our old cloth'n 'long in case we r'turned today."

"He—I think he robbed the A'alude's treas'ry 'fore he joined us." PRudenCe's voice was faint; her eyes were very bright, as if she were holding back tears.

In the gloom of the attic, UNison's face had a grayish cast; his arms tightened around his bundle, and he looked around wildly, as if searching for a way to escape.

"You only have a few seconds to make up your mind, Cit'zen UNison," ConCord said coldly. "There's no way you can get any pers'nal ben'fit from that gold. It's too precious for even the black market to handle. Someone is sure to b'tray you, and then the gold will be seized by the State—and you'll have noth'n. But if you turn it over to AMitY now so she can r'turn it to E'ewere, you'll still have a mid-stat 'signment at Grissom House, as I promised."

UNison's mouth twisted into an ugly line. It was

more than the few seconds ConCord had allotted him before he finally shrugged. "I'll hold you to your promise, Cit'zen ConCord-Grissom," he said sullenly; again, it sounded like a threat.

Silently, AMitY took the bundle from him. It was very heavy, and she wondered which of the A'aludes' treasures he had stolen. How had he intended to dispose of them—or had he thought that far ahead? Without special permits, private citizens were forbidden to own common metals like iron and steel, much less something as valuable as gold. Perhaps, as ConCord suspected, UNison had planned to sell it on the black market that everybody knew existed in the Idles and Artisan Swarms. Well, he'd been thwarted in his plans, whatever they had been; but how long would a mid-status job as a Museum House steward satisfy him? What if, in his greed, he decided that he could derive more personal benefit for himself by going to the authorities with his story?

Deeply troubled, she turned to the window. In an effort to blot out everything but the necessity of summoning up the Portal, she closed her eyes.

Even so, it was difficult to concentrate now. Already E'ewere seemed unreal, a shadow world. Only her own world, with its problems—and its promise— was real. And if reality was here in this dusty attic with the people she loved, then what was E'ewere? A delusion? In time, would she lose the ability to call up the Portal?

She put aside her personal concerns, knowing that she would return to them later, and let her mind fill with images of E'ewere. The sullen light against her closed eyelids took on a bluish cast, and when she opened her eyes, the four blue moons of E'ewere were overhead. For a long moment she drank in their beauty.

Behind her, someone moved restlessly, reminding her that she was wasting time. She slung the square of silk that held the A'alude's gold over her shoulder and slipped through the window.

A flash of cold .. . a searing heat that prickled her skin ... nausea ... all so familiar now. For a too-long moment, she stared into a hideous world of discordant, garish colors. But before the fear she felt had time to mature to panic, the gaudy oranges and reds faded into the cool blues of a E'ewere evening.

It surprised her that everything was the same as she'd left it a few minutes earlier. But then—what had she expected? That the A'aludes would have come here to mourn their guests' return to their own world?

No, she couldn't expect that. No matter how kind they had been to her, they would be glad to be rid of their disruptive guests. What kind of legends would this latest visit from humankind evoke? Would UNison's avarice become a scary legend to be told around the hearth when the wind howled at the corners of their snug cottages?

And what about her? Would they forget her mistakes and only remember that she had loved them? And HUmble—would Dl'lark and Wocho pass down their own legends about their friend, keeping his memory green in the valley of the A'aludes?

She sighed, and with the sigh, relinquished all claim to the world that belonged to the A'aludes. She laid down the bundle of silk that held the stolen gold, but she didn't leave yet.

She closed her eyes, sure that she heard the sweet sad keening voices of the A'aludes. That they would make the passing of the elders an occasion for singing didn't surprise her—but perhaps, by extending the lives of their elders a few more years, she could give them a reason for singing a happier song.

She folded her arms across her chest and bowed her head, unconsciously assuming the Stance for Meditation. She let her thoughts float free, filling her mind with images of Queen Aur'ri: her fair, feathery hair, her wings of lavender-ombre, her luminous eyes. When she felt a quickening deep inside, as if someone had said her name, she spoke of her gratitude, of her regret.

"Guard the Portal, and if 'nother like me comes, turn him back," she said. "Don't be fooled 'cause he has a gentle manner or 'cause the color of his hair matches your legends. 'Beware of Man, for *he* is the Troggo,' are the words the Sojourner carved into the stones, and they speak Truth. Your enemy is Man. It was Man who drove you from your first refuge, from Earth."

She sensed sorrow, but not surprise, and then a tingling, as if Queen Aur'ri's hand, with its fragile bones, had touched her cheek, and a bell-like voice echoed through her mind.

"From the beginning, we have known the face of our enemy—but it is not your face, Our Lady AMitY. You came as a friend, and you leave as a friend. Farewell, Our Lady AMitY. Live long and live with purpose."

The voice in AMitY's mind faded, and she was alone again. She turned back to the Portal. For a long time, she stared down at the small crystal dome that protruded from its frame, preparing herself. There was one more task to perform. Only a clear mind, she knew, one free of doubt, could accomplish the thing she must do, and yet—her mind seethed with unrest, with tiny threads of fear and regret.

One of the Litanies came to her, the one taught to children during their third year of school.

When I am troubled, let Peace be my friend.
Let it guide my conscience and ease my mind,
So that I may act for the good of all.
And when duty rests heaviest upon my shoulders,
Let Peace fill my mind and be my friend. . . .

When she was ready, she laid her hand on the small crystal dome. It radiated a warmth that was oddly comforting, as if it were assuring her that she was doing the right thing.

And what if she were stranded here forever—or was trapped on one of the alien worlds of the Portal, trying to return to her own people? What if she never saw her family or ConCord or another human being again? Would she still feel that she had done the right thing?

Suddenly impatient with her own vacillating, she shook off the lingering doubts and concentrated on the small glittering dome. It began to pulsate, to glow, as if waiting her command.

"Close the Portal," she said, speaking the words aloud, although she knew it wasn't necessary.

At first, when nothing happened, she thought she had failed; and then the dome began to pulsate faster and the glow increased. Inside the Portal, the gray mist swirled in dizzy circles, and she knew that she had succeeded.

She sprang forward then, not giving herself time to think, and plunged, head first, into a diminishing square of gray mist. Then she was falling—upward,